ANDERSEN'S
FAIRY TALES

Retold by Friederun Reichenstetter
Illustrated by Silke Leffler

NORTHSOUTH
BOOKS

New York / London

"LIFE ITSELF IS THE MOST WONDERFUL FAIRY TALE."

—HANS CHRISTIAN ANDERSEN

The Princess and the Pea, *The Emperor's New Clothes*, *The Tinderbox*,
The Little Match Girl, *The Swineherd*, and *Thumbeline* were translated by Anthea Bell.

The Ugly Duckling, *The Traveling Companion*, *There is No Doubt*, *The Sweethearts*, *The Steadfast Tin Soldier*,
The Flying Trunk, and *Jack the Dullard* were adapted for this book from translations by H.P. Paul.

Copyright © 2004 by Annette Betz Verlag, Vienna, Austria, and Munich, Germany
First published in Austria under the title *Das Andersen Märchenbuch*
English translation copyright © 2007 by North-South Books Inc., New York

First published in the United States, Great Britain, Canada, Australia, and New Zealand in 2007 by North-South Books Inc., an imprint
of NordSüd Verlag AG, Zürich, Switzerland. Distributed in the United States by North-South Books Inc., New York.

Library of Congress Cataloging-in-Publication Data is available.
A CIP catalogue record for this book is available from The British Library.

ISBN-13: 978-0-7358-2141-5 / ISBN-10: 0-7358-2141-0 (trade edition)
10 9 8 7 6 5 4 3 2 1

Printed in Belgium

Published in cooperation with Annette Betz Verlag, Vienna, Munich

www.northsouth.com

CONTENTS

THE PRINCESS AND THE PEA

ONCE UPON A TIME, there was a prince who wanted to marry a princess, but she had to be a real princess. So he went all around the world looking for one, but there was something the matter everywhere. He met plenty of princesses, but he couldn't be sure whether they were real princesses. There was always something not quite right about them. So he came home again, feeling very sad, because he did so want to marry a real princess.

One evening, there was a terrible storm, with thunder and lightning and rain pouring down. It was really dreadful! Someone came knocking at the great gate, and the old king went to open it.

There was a princess standing outside, but, oh dear, she was in such a state with the rain and the terrible storm! Water was dripping from her hair and her clothes, running in at the toes of her shoes and out at the heels again. But she said she was a real princess.

Well, thought the old queen, we'll soon see about that! However, she said nothing but went into the bedroom, took all the bedclothes off, and put a pea on the bedstead. Then she took twenty mattresses and put them on top of the pea, and after that she put twenty eiderdown quilts on top of the mattresses. That was where the princess was to spend the night.

In the morning the princess was asked how she had slept.

"Oh, very badly!" said the princess. "I could hardly sleep a wink all night! Goodness knows what was in my bed! I was lying on something so hard that I'm black and blue all over. It's really terrible!"

So then they could tell she was a real princess, because she had felt the pea through all twenty mattresses and twenty eiderdown quilts. Only a real princess could be as sensitive as that.

The prince married her, for now he knew he had found a real princess, and the pea was put in a museum, where it can be seen to this day, if nobody has taken it.

There, that was a real story!

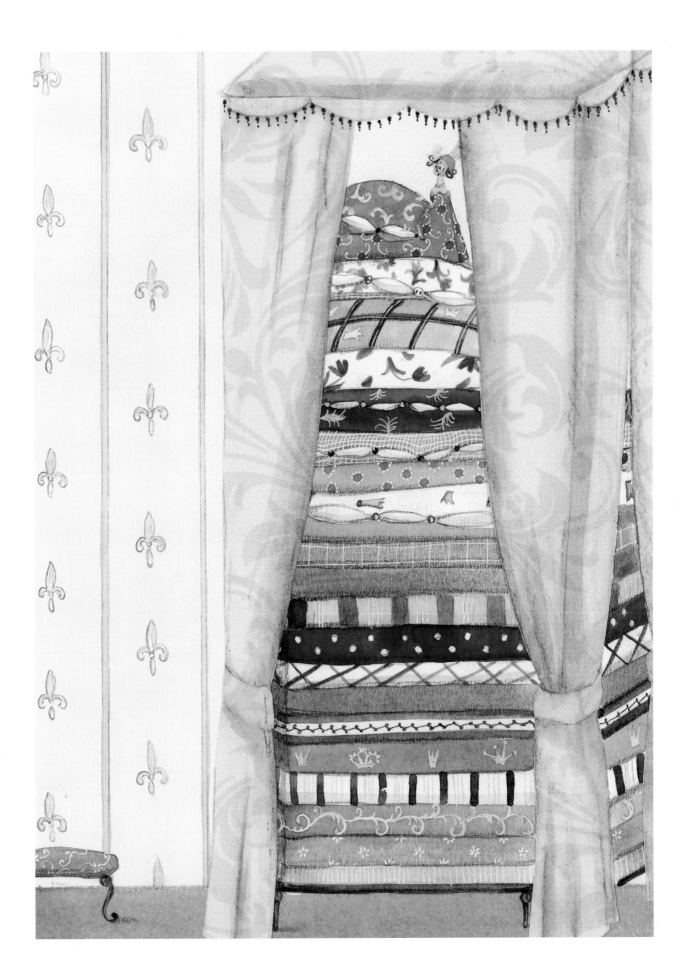

THE EMPEROR'S NEW CLOTHES

MANY YEARS AGO, there was an emperor who thought fine new clothes were so important that he spent all his money on them. He did not care about his army or going to the theater or hunting in the forest, except as opportunities to show off his new clothes. He had a different suit for every time of the day, and while people will often say of a king, "He is in the council chamber," they said of this emperor, "He is in his dressing room."

The great city where he lived was a prosperous place, and many visitors came daily to see it. One day, however, two rascally swindlers arrived in town, pretending to be weavers and claiming to make the most beautiful cloth you could imagine. Not only were the colors and patterns of the cloth amazingly lovely, they said, but clothes made of it had the wonderful property of remaining invisible to anyone who was either unfit for his job or remarkably stupid.

Those must be marvelous clothes indeed, thought the emperor. If I wore them I could find out which people in my land are unfit for the positions they hold. I could tell who was clever and who was stupid! I must have that cloth made for me at once!

And he gave the two swindlers a great deal of money to begin work. So they set up two looms and pretended to be working, but, in fact, were not weaving at all. They said they needed the finest silk and the most precious gold thread, all of which they pocketed themselves, and they worked at their empty looms until late into the night.

I wonder how my cloth is coming along, thought the emperor. He felt slightly

alarmed when he remembered that a stupid man, or one unfit for his position, wouldn't be able to see it. He didn't think he need fear for himself, but all the same, he decided to send someone else to see how the work was going.

All the people in town knew about the wonderful powers of the cloth, and they were all eager to find out how clever or how stupid their neighbors were.

I'll send my honest old minister to call on the weavers, thought the emperor. He's the best person to see what the cloth looks like, for he is very clever, and no one could be better fitted for his post!

Well, the good old minister went into the hall where the two swindlers were sitting, working at their empty looms. Lord preserve us! thought the old minister, opening his eyes very wide. I can't see anything at all! But he didn't say so.

The two swindlers asked him to be so good as to come closer. Wasn't the pattern very fine, they asked, and weren't the colors beautiful? As they spoke they pointed to the empty loom, and the poor old minister kept staring, but he could see nothing at all, since there was nothing there. Dear me! he thought. Can it be that I'm stupid? Am I unfit for my post? I never thought so myself. Well, no one must know of this!

"Haven't you anything to say?" asked one of the swindlers, pretending to go on weaving.

"Oh yes, it's very nice! Really splendid!" said the old minister, peering through his glasses. "That pattern! Those colors! Yes, I'll tell the emperor I like it very much indeed!"

"Delighted to hear it!" said the two weavers, and then they told him what the colors were and described the unusual pattern. The old minister listened carefully so that he could tell the emperor all about it, and so he did.

Then the two swindlers asked for more money and more silk and gold thread, saying they needed it for the weaving. They put it all into their own pockets again and went on weaving at their looms, which were as empty as ever.

Soon the emperor sent another honest officer of state to see how the weaving was getting on and find out if the cloth would soon be ready. Like the minister

before him, the officer of state looked and looked, but as there was nothing on the empty looms, he couldn't see anything either.

"Isn't it a fine piece of cloth?" said the two swindlers, and they pretended to show it to him, describing the beautiful pattern, which wasn't there at all.

I'm sure I'm not stupid, thought the officer of state. So I must be unfit for my job! Well, this is a strange thing, indeed, and I mustn't let anyone know about it!

So he praised the cloth he couldn't see, saying how much he liked the fine colors and the beautiful pattern. "Yes, it really is quite exquisite!" he told the emperor.

All the people in town were talking about that wonderful cloth. So now the emperor wanted to see it for himself while it was still on the loom. He called on the cunning swindlers with a very select company of courtiers, including the two good old gentlemen who had been to see the cloth before. The two rascals were weaving away with all their might, although there wasn't a single thread on the loom.

"Isn't it superb?" said the minister and the officer of state. "Oh, Your Majesty, just see the pattern and those colors!" And they pointed to the empty loom, believing that everyone else really could see the cloth.

Goodness me! thought the emperor. I can't see anything at all! This is terrible! Am I stupid? Am I unfit to be emperor? This is the worst thing that could possibly happen to me! However, he said out loud, "Oh yes, it's very beautiful! I like it very much indeed!" And he nodded approvingly at the empty loom. He didn't want to admit that he could see nothing at all.

All the courtiers with him stared and stared too, but they couldn't see any more than the minister and the officer of state. However, they copied the emperor and said, "Really, most attractive!" And they advised him to have the wonderful new cloth made into a suit of clothes to wear in the great procession that was soon to take place. The word went from one to another. "Superb!" "Exquisite!" "Excellent!" The courtiers all said how much they liked the cloth, and the emperor gave the two swindlers decorations to wear in their buttonholes and dubbed them knights of the loom.

The two rascally swindlers sat up all night before the day of the procession, with sixteen lights burning, and everyone could see how hard they were working to have

the emperor's new clothes ready in time. They pretended to be taking the cloth off the looms, they snipped their scissors in empty air, they sewed busily away using needles without any thread. Finally they said, "Look, the clothes are ready!"

The emperor himself arrived, with his most distinguished courtiers, and the two swindlers raised their arms in the air as if they were holding something. "Look, here are the trousers!" they said. "And here's the coat! And here's the cloak! It's as light as a cobweb! You might think you were wearing nothing at all, but that's the whole beauty of these clothes!"

"Yes, to be sure!" said all the courtiers, although they still couldn't see anything, because there was nothing to be seen.

"Will Your Imperial Majesty be so gracious as to take your clothes off?" asked the swindlers. "Then we'll dress you in your new ones over there by the big mirror!"

So the emperor took off all his clothes, and the two swindlers pretended to be dressing him in the new ones they were supposed to have made, fitting them around his waist and acting as if they were putting on the train, while the emperor turned around and preened in front of the mirror.

"Oh, how fine those clothes are!" said everyone. "What a perfect fit! What a pattern! What colors! That's a splendid suit of clothes indeed!"

"The canopy to be carried over you in the procession is waiting outside," said the master of ceremonies.

"I'm ready!" said the emperor. "Don't my clothes suit me well?" And he twisted and turned in front of the mirror once more, pretending to be admiring his fine clothes. The chamberlains who were to carry the train fumbled on the floor as if they were picking it up and then pretended to be carrying it. They were afraid to let anyone notice that they couldn't see a thing.

So the emperor walked in the procession under the fine canopy, and all the people in the streets and standing at the windows cried, "Oh, how wonderful the emperor's new clothes look! What a fine cloak he's wearing over his coat! How well they suit him!" For no one wanted people to think he couldn't see anything. That

would have meant he was either stupid or unfit for his job. None of the emperor's other clothes had ever been so greatly admired.

"But the emperor has no clothes on!" said a child.

"Listen to the little innocent!" said the child's father. And the people began passing what the child had said on to each other.

"The emperor has no clothes on! The child over there says the emperor has no clothes on!"

Finally all the people were shouting, "The emperor has no clothes on!" And the emperor cringed, for he thought in his heart they were right, but he said to himself, "I must hold out until the end of the procession." So he bore himself even more proudly than before, and the chamberlains went on carrying that train that wasn't there at all.

THE TINDERBOX

A SOLDIER came marching down the high road. *One, two! One, two!* He had his knapsack on his back and a sword at his side, for he had been away fighting in the wars, and now he was going home.

As he went along, he met an old witch on the road. She was very ugly, with a lower lip that hung down to her chest.

"Good evening, soldier!" said she. "What a fine sword you have and what a big knapsack! I see you are a real soldier indeed. Well now, you can have as much money as you want!"

"Thank you kindly, old witch," said the soldier.

"Do you see that big tree?" asked the witch, pointing to a tree growing near the road. "It's hollow inside! Climb up it and you will see the hole. You can get into that hole and right down inside the tree. I'll tie a rope around your waist, and then I can haul you up when you call me!"

"But what am I to do inside the tree?" asked the soldier.

"Fetch the money!" said the witch. "When you reach the bottom of the tree, you will find yourself in a great passage. It is very light, for there are over a hundred lamps burning there. You'll see three doors. You can open them, for the keys are in the locks. Go into the first room, and in the middle of the floor you will see a large chest with a dog sitting on it. He has eyes as big as teacups, but don't let that alarm you. I'll give you my blue-checked apron. Just spread it on the floor, and then you can march up to the dog, place him on the apron, open the chest, and take as much money out of it as you like. The coins in that chest are all copper, but if you would rather have silver, then go into the next room, where you will find a dog with eyes as big as mill wheels. However, don't let that alarm you. Just put him on the apron and take the money! And if you would rather have gold, go into the third room and take as much of it as you can carry. The dog sitting on the chest of money in the third room has eyes as big as the Round Tower of Copenhagen. He's a remarkable dog and no mistake! But don't let that alarm you. Just put him on the apron. He won't touch you, and you can take as much gold as you like out of the chest!"

"That sounds like a pretty good notion!" said the soldier. "But what am I to give you in return, old witch? I'm sure you must want something for yourself!"

"No," said the witch, "not a single coin. I just want you to bring me the old tinderbox my grandmother forgot when she was last down there."

"Well, tie the rope around my waist, then!" said the soldier.

"Here it is," said the witch, "and here's my blue-checked apron."

So the soldier climbed the tree and let himself down into the hollow trunk.

There he was in the great passage with over a hundred lamps burning, exactly as the witch had said.

He opened the first door—and there sat the dog with eyes as big as teacups, glaring at him.

"Nice doggy!" said the soldier, putting him on the witch's apron. He filled his pockets with all the copper coins he could carry, closed the chest, put the dog back on top of it, and went into the next room.

My word! There sat the dog with eyes as big as mill wheels.

"Don't you stare at me like that!" said the soldier. "You might do your eyes an injury!" And he put the dog on the witch's apron. When he saw all the silver coins in the chest, he threw away the copper he had taken and filled his pockets and his knapsack with pure silver. Then he went on into the third room. That was an alarming sight and no mistake! The dog in there really did have eyes as big as the Round Tower, and they went around and around in his head like wheels.

"Good evening to you," said the soldier, touching his cap respectfully to the dog, for he had never seen such an animal before. He stood and gaped at him for a while, but then he thought, Well, that's enough of that! And he picked the dog up, put him on the apron, and opened the chest.

Mercy, what a lot of gold it held! Enough to buy the whole of Copenhagen and the sweetmeat sellers' sugar pigs, enough to buy all the tin soldiers and toy whips and rocking horses in the world. This was wealth indeed!

So the soldier emptied his pockets and knapsack of all the silver coins and filled them with gold instead—his pockets, his knapsack, even his cap and boots, so that he could hardly walk. He had plenty of money now! He put the dog back on the chest, closed the door, and called up through the hollow tree, "You can haul me up, old witch!"

"Have you found the tinderbox?" asked the witch.

"My word!" said the soldier. "I forgot all about it!" So he went back and found it. Then the witch hauled him up, and there he was, standing on the high road again, with his pockets, his boots, his knapsack, and his cap full of money.

"What do you want the tinderbox for?" asked the soldier.

"Mind your own business," said the witch. "You have your money, so hand over the tinderbox!"

"None of that, now!" said the soldier. "You tell me what you want the tinderbox for or I'll draw my sword and cut off your head."

"I won't!" said the witch.

So the soldier cut off her head, and there she lay. He tied up all his money in her apron, slung the bundle over his back, put the tinderbox in his pocket, and marched on to the nearest town.

It was a very fine town, and he went into the grandest inn, hired the best room, and ordered his favorite food, for he had so much money that he was a rich man now.

The servant who cleaned the shoes thought it strange that a rich man should wear such shabby old boots, but the soldier hadn't had time to get any new ones yet. Next day, however, he bought boots and clothes fit for a fine gentleman, and the townsfolk told him all about their town and their king and what a lovely girl his daughter, the princess, was.

"How can I see her?" asked the soldier.

"Oh, no one can see her!" said the townsfolk. "She lives in a great copper castle surrounded by walls and towers. The king won't let anyone see her but himself, because it has been foretold that she will marry a common soldier, and the king doesn't care for that idea at all."

The soldier thought, I'd like to see her all the same. But there was no chance he could do that.

Well, the soldier lived a merry life. He went to the theater, he drove out in the king's park, and he also gave a great deal of money to the poor, for he remembered what it was like to be penniless. Now that he was rich and wore fine clothes, he made a great many friends. They all said he was a good fellow and a real gentleman. That was the kind of thing the soldier liked to hear!

However, he was spending money every day, but no more money was coming in, so he was soon down to his last two coins. He had to move out of the grand room where he had been living to take a little one in the attic. He brushed and mended his own boots now, and none of his friends came to see him anymore. There were so many stairs to climb.

One dark evening, when he could not even afford to buy a candle, he remembered that there was a little candle end in the tinderbox he had fetched for the old witch from the hollow tree. He found the tinderbox and the candle end, but as soon as he struck a spark from the flint, the door flew open and in came the dog he had seen in the passage below the tree, the dog with eyes as big as teacups. He stopped in front of the soldier.

"What are your orders, master?" said the dog.

"Upon my word!" said the soldier. "This is a remarkable tinderbox if it means I can order anything I want! Fetch me some money!" he said, and the dog was gone in a twinkling. Next moment he was back again, with a great bag of coins in his mouth. Now the soldier realized what a wonderful tinderbox he had! If he struck the flint once, the dog from the chest of copper coins appeared; if he struck it twice, the dog from the chest of silver came; and if he struck it three times, the dog from the chest of gold coins arrived. So the soldier went back to live in his grand room again and wore fine clothes, and his friends all remembered him and made a great fuss over him. Well, one day he was thinking, what a pity it is that no one can see the princess! Everyone says she's so beautiful, but what's the good of that if she's always kept shut up in a copper castle surrounded by towers? Can't I find some way to see her? Where's my tinderbox? He struck the flint, and in came the dog with eyes as big as teacups.

"I know it's the middle of the night," said the soldier, "but I would so like to see the princess, just for a moment!"

The dog went straight out of the door, and before the soldier knew it, he was back with the princess riding on him, still fast asleep. She was so pretty that anyone could see she was a real princess, and the soldier, who was a real soldier, could not help kissing her. Then the dog took the princess home again. But in the morning, when the king and queen were drinking tea, she told them that she had dreamed a very strange dream that night, about a dog and a soldier. In her dream she rode the dog's back and the soldier kissed her.

"Dear me, what a story!" said the queen.

And one of the old ladies-in-waiting was told to keep watch by the princess' bedside the next night, to see if it was really a dream or not.

The soldier longed to see the beautiful princess again, and so the dog came for 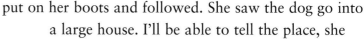 her in the night. He ran as fast as could, but the old lady-in-waiting put on her boots and followed. She saw the dog go into a large house. I'll be able to tell the place, she thought, and she took a piece of chalk and drew a cross on the door. Then she went home and lay down, and the dog soon brought the princess back.

But noticing the cross drawn on the door of the soldier's inn, the dog took a piece of chalk too, and drew a cross on every other door in town. That was very clever, because now that all the doors had crosses on them, the lady-in-waiting couldn't find the right one.

Early in the morning the king, the queen, the old lady-in-waiting, and all the courtiers went to see where the princess had been.

"That's it!" said the king, seeing the first door with a cross on it.

"No, my dear, it's this one!" said the queen, looking at the next door, which also had a cross on it.

"It's this one! No, it's this one!" said everyone. But wherever they looked there were crosses on the doors, so they couldn't tell which one they really wanted.

However, the queen was a very clever woman who would do more than sit in a state carriage. She took her golden scissors, cut up a piece of silk, and made a pretty little bag of it. She

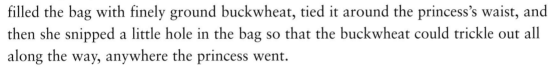

filled the bag with finely ground buckwheat, tied it around the princess's waist, and then she snipped a little hole in the bag so that the buckwheat could trickle out all along the way, anywhere the princess went.

The dog came again that night, took the princess on his back, and carried her off to the soldier. He was so much in love with her that he wished he were a prince and could have her for his wife.

But the dog never noticed the buckwheat trickling out all the way from the castle to the place where he jumped up on the wall with the princess and in through the soldier's window. Next morning the king and queen could tell where their daughter had been, and the soldier was arrested and put in prison.

So there he sat. It was dark and dreary, and they told him he was to be hanged the next day. That was not at all amusing, and he had left the tinderbox in his room at the inn.

In the morning, through the iron bars of the little window of his cell, he could see people hurrying out of the town to the place of execution to see him hanged. He heard drums and saw guards marching by.

All the people were going out to see the show. Among the crowd there was a cobbler's apprentice in his leather apron and slippers, running so fast that one of the slippers flew off and fell to the ground near the wall of the prison, where the soldier was peering out through the iron bars.

"Hey, you, cobbler's boy! Don't be in such a hurry," called the soldier. "Nothing's going to happen until I get there! Listen, if you go to the inn where I was staying and fetch me my tinderbox, I'll give you four coins, but you must hurry!"

Well, the cobbler's apprentice wanted to earn four coins, so he ran off to fetch the tinderbox, gave it to the soldier, and then—yes, now we'll see what happened!

A gallows had been set up outside the town. It was surrounded by guards and hundreds of thousands of people. The king and the queen were sitting on a grand throne, with the judge and the whole council opposite.

The soldier had already climbed the ladder, but when they were going to put the noose around his neck, he said it was usual for a condemned man to be granted one last wish before he died. He would very much like to smoke a pipe of tobacco, he said, the last pipe he would ever smoke in this world.

The king could hardly refuse him, so the soldier brought out his tinderbox and struck the flint—once, twice, three times. And there were all the dogs: the dog with eyes as big as teacups, the dog with eyes as big as mill wheels, and the dog with eyes as big as the Round Tower of Copenhagen.

"Come along, help me. I don't want to be hanged!" said the soldier, and the dogs raced toward the judge and the council, seizing one man by the leg and another by the nose, and tossed them all so high into the air that when they came down they broke into pieces.

"Leave me alone!" said the king, but the biggest dog seized him and the queen and tossed them up in the air too, after all the others. The guards were terrified, and all the people shouted, "Little soldier, we want you to be our king and marry the beautiful princess!"

So the soldier drove in the king's carriage, and all three dogs pranced in front of it. Boys whistled and the guards presented their arms. The princess came out of her copper castle and became queen, and she liked that very much indeed! The wedding festivities went on for a week, and the dogs sat at the table with the other guests, staring around them with their great big eyes.

THE UGLY DUCKLING

IT WAS a lovely summer day in the country. In a sunny spot stood a pleasant old farmhouse next to a river. Tall reeds and bushes grew from the house all the way down to the water's edge. In this snug retreat sat a duck on her nest, waiting for her eggs to hatch. She was beginning to get tired of her task, for the ducklings were taking their time coming out of their shells.

Finally, one shell cracked, and then another, and from each egg came a tiny creature that lifted its head and cried, "*Peep, Peep*!"

"*Quack, quack*!" said Mother. Then they looked around at the large green leaves that surrounded the nest. "How large the world is," they said, when they saw how much more room there was outside their eggshells.

"Do you think this is the whole world?" asked Mother. "Wait until you see the garden. It stretches all the way to the parson's field, but I have never ventured to such a distance. Are you all out?" she continued, rising. "No, the largest egg is still lying there. How much longer will it be till this last egg hatches? I am quite tired of it." She sat down again on the nest.

"Well, how are you getting on?" asked an old duck, who came to pay her a visit.

"One egg still has not hatched," said the duck, "but look at all the others, aren't they the prettiest little ducklings you ever saw?"

"Let me see that egg," said the duck. "It might be a turkey's egg. I was persuaded to hatch some once, and after all my care and trouble with the young ones, they were afraid of the water. I quacked and clucked, but all to no purpose. I could not get them to go in. Let me look at the egg. Yes, that's a turkey's egg; take my advice, leave it where it is and teach the other children to swim."

"I think I'll sit on it a little while longer," said the duck. "I have sat so long already, a few more days will be nothing."

"Please yourself," said the old duck, and she went away.

At last the large egg broke, and a duckling crept out crying, "*Peep, Peep*!" It was very large and ugly. The mother duck stared at it and exclaimed, "It is very large and not at all like the others. I wonder if it really is a turkey. We shall soon find out when we go to the water. It will go in, even if I have to push it in myself."

The next day the weather was delightful. The sun shone brightly, so the mother duck took her young brood down to the water and jumped in with a splash. "*Quack, quack,*" she cried, and one after another the little ducklings jumped in. The water closed over their heads, but they came up again in an instant, and swam about quite prettily, their tiny legs paddling under them. The ugly duckling was also in the water swimming.

"Oh," said the mother, "he is not a turkey; look how well he uses his legs, and how straight he holds himself! He is my child, and he is not so very ugly if you look at him properly. *Quack, quack!* Come with me now, I will take you to the farmyard, but you must keep close to me and, above all, beware of the cat. Come, now, use your legs, and let me see how well you can behave. Don't turn your toes, a well-bred duckling spreads his feet wide apart like this. Now bend your neck, and say *quack.*"

The little ducklings did as they were told, but the other ducks stared, and said, "Look, here comes another brood and what a queer-looking duckling that one is. We don't want him here." One flew out and bit him on the neck.

"Leave him alone," said Mother.

"But he is so big and ugly," said the spiteful duck. "He doesn't belong here."

"The others are very pretty," said an old duck with a rag on her leg. "All but that one."

"He is not pretty; but he has a very good disposition," replied Mother, "and he swims as well or even better than the others. I think he will grow up fine. He just stayed in his egg too long." And she stroked his neck and smoothed his feathers, saying, "He is a drake, so it doesn't matter. I think he will grow up strong and able to take care of himself."

"The other ducklings are graceful enough," said the old duck. "Now make yourself at home."

And so they made themselves comfortable; but the ugly duckling was bitten and pushed and made fun of, not only by the ducks, but also by the chickens and turkeys. "He is too big," they all said. The turkey cock strutted about like he was a king. He fancied himself to be quite important. Suddenly he would puff up his chest and fly at the duckling. The poor little thing didn't know where to go, and he was miserable because he was so ugly. The whole farmyard laughed at him. Day after day, the poor little ugly duckling was chased about by everyone. Even his brothers and sisters were mean to him.

The ducks pecked him, the chickens beat him, and the girl who fed the poultry kicked him with her feet. So at last he ran away.

"They are afraid of me because I am ugly," he thought as he flew. He closed his eyes and flew until he came to a large lake inhabited by wild ducks where he stopped to spend the night. He was very tired and very sad.

In the morning, when the wild ducks rose in the air, they stared at the new duck. "What sort of a duck are you?" they all said, swimming around him.

He bowed and was as polite as he could be, but he did not reply to their question. "You are exceedingly ugly," said the wild ducks.

Poor thing! All he wanted was to rest among the reeds. After he had been there for a few days, he was out in the water swimming when suddenly, *pop, pop!* sounded in the air. *Pop, pop!* echoed far and wide as whole flocks of wild ducks filled the sky. The sound came from every direction, for hunters had surrounded the lake. Some were even seated on the branches of trees. Blue smoke from their guns rose like clouds as it floated away. Across the water, a dog bounded through the rushes. He terrified the ugly duckling! He turned his head and hid it under his wing just as the large, terrible dog passed by. The dog's jaws were open, his tongue hung from his mouth, and his eyes glared. He thrust his nose close to the duckling, showing his sharp teeth, and then, *splash, splash,* he went into the water without touching him.

"Oh," sighed the duckling, "thank goodness I am so ugly that even a dog doesn't want to bite me." He lay quite still, while the shots rattled through the rushes, and gun after gun was fired over him. It was late in the day before all became quiet again, but the poor ugly duckling didn't dare move. He waited quietly for hours, and then, after looking around carefully, he hurried away from the lake as fast as he could. He ran over field and meadow till a storm arose. Toward evening, he reached a poor little cottage that seemed ready to fall over and only remained standing because it could not decide which way to fall first. The violent storm continued. The ugly duckling could go no farther and sat down by the cottage. He noticed that the door didn't quite close because one of the hinges had broken. There was a narrow opening near the bottom just large enough for him to slip through, which he did very quietly. A woman, a tomcat, and a hen lived in this cottage. The woman called the tomcat her *little son*, as he was her favorite. He could raise his back and purr. He could even make sparks fly from his fur if you stroked him the wrong way. The hen had very short legs, so she was called *chickie short legs*. She laid good eggs, and the woman loved her as if she were her own child. In the morning, their ugly visitor was discovered, and the tomcat began to purr, and the hen began to cluck.

"What is all that noise about?" asked the old woman, looking around the room, but her sight was not very good. When she saw the duckling she thought he must be a fat duck that had strayed from home. "Oh, how wonderful!"

she cried. "I hope it is not a drake, for then I shall have some duck's eggs. I must wait and see." So the duckling was allowed to remain on trial for three weeks, but there were no eggs.

Now the tomcat, who was the master of the house, and the hen, who was mistress, believed themselves to be half the world, and the better half at that.

The duckling thought that others might hold a different opinion on the subject, but the hen would not listen to such doubts.

"Can you lay eggs?" she asked. "No? Then have the goodness to hold your tongue."

"Can you raise your back, or purr, or throw out sparks?" queried the tomcat. "No? Then you have no right to express an opinion when sensible people are speaking."

So the ugly duckling sat in a corner, feeling very low. When the sunshine and fresh air poured into the room through the door, he began to feel a longing for a swim on the water.

"What an absurd idea," said the hen. "You have nothing else to do, so you have foolish fancies. If you could purr or lay eggs, they would pass away."

"But it is so delightful to swim about on the water," said the duckling, "and so refreshing to feel it close over your head, when you dive down to the bottom."

"Delightful, indeed!" said the hen. "Why you must be crazy! Ask the cat, he is the cleverest animal I know. Ask him how he would like to swim about on the water or to dive under it, for I will not speak of my own opinion. Ask our mistress, the old woman—there is no one in the world more clever than she. Do you think she would like to swim or to let the water close over her head?"

"You just don't understand," said the duckling.

"We don't understand you? Who can understand you, I wonder? Do you consider yourself cleverer than the cat or the old woman? I will say nothing of myself. Such nonsense, child! You should thank your good fortune that we let you stay here. Are you not in a warm room with companions from whom you may learn something? But you do nothing but chatter and your company is not very agreeable. Believe me, I say this for your own good. I may tell you unpleasant truths, but that is a proof of my friendship. I advise you to lay eggs and learn to purr as quickly as possible."

"I believe I must go out into the world again," said the duckling.

"Go then," said the hen. So the ugly duckling left the cottage and soon found water on which he could swim and dive, but the other animals avoided him because of his ugly appearance. Autumn came, and the leaves in the forest turned to orange and gold. Then, as winter approached, the wind caught them and they whirled in the cold air. The clouds, heavy with hail and snowflakes, hung low in the sky, and the raven stood on the ferns crying, "*Cawww, cawww!*" It made one shiver with cold to look at him. The poor little ugly duckling was so sad. One evening, just as the sun was setting amid radiant clouds, a large flock of beautiful birds flew over the lake. The duckling had never seen birds like these before. They were swans. They curved their graceful necks while their soft, white feathers glistened. They uttered a singular cry as they spread their glorious wings and flew higher and higher in the air. The ugly duckling felt a strange sensation as he watched them. He whirled in the water like a wheel, stretched out his neck toward them, and uttered a cry so strange that it frightened him. He would never forget those beautiful, happy birds. When at last they were out of his sight, he dived under the water, and rose again almost beside himself with excitement.

"If only I were as lovely as they are," he wished. The winter grew colder and colder. He had to swim around in the water to keep from freezing. Every night, the space in the water where he swam became smaller and smaller. Soon it froze so hard that the ice in the water crackled as he moved, and the ugly duckling had to paddle as hard as he could to keep his space from closing up entirely.

Early the next morning, a farmer who was passing by saw him and carried the duckling home to his wife. The warmth of the fire revived the poor little duckling. But when the children wanted to play with him, the duckling was startled and jumped up in terror. He fluttered into the milk pan, splashing the milk around the room. Then the woman clapped her hands, which frightened him even more. The woman screamed and waved her broom at him while the children laughed. They tumbled over one another as they tried to catch him. The door was open and the ugly duckling managed to slip out. He flew to the bushes where he lay down in the newly fallen snow. Winter was long and cold for the ugly duckling.

Finally, winter was over. The ugly duckling felt the warm sun shining and heard the lark singing. It was spring! The young bird's wings were now strong, and he flapped them against his sides, rising high into the air. The apple trees were in full bloom, and the fragrant elders bent their long green branches down to the stream that wound around a smooth lawn. Everything looked beautiful in the freshness of early spring. From a thicket close by came three beautiful white swans, rustling their feathers and swimming lightly over the smooth water. The duckling remembered the lovely birds and felt lonelier than ever.

"I will fly to those birds," he exclaimed. "They will kill me because I am so ugly, but it does not matter. Better to be killed by them than pecked by the ducks, beaten by the hens, pushed about by the girl who feeds the poultry, or starved with hunger in the winter."

He flew down to the water and swam toward the beautiful swans. The moment they saw him, they rushed to him with outstretched wings. He bent his head down to the surface of the water and waited for them to attack. But what did he see in the clear stream below? His own image. He was no longer a dark, gray bird, ugly and disagreeable to look at, but a graceful and beautiful swan. To be born in a duck's nest, in a farmyard, is of no consequence to a bird, if it is hatched from a swan's egg. He now felt glad at having suffered sorrow and trouble, because it enabled him to enjoy so much more all the pleasure and happiness around him. The great swans swam round the newcomer and welcomed him by stroking his neck with their beaks.

Some little children came to the lake and threw bread and cake into the water.

"Look," cried the youngest, "there is a new one." And the rest were delighted and ran to their father and mother, dancing and clapping their hands and shouting happily, "There is another swan—a new one has arrived!"

Then they threw more bread and cake into the water and said, "The new one is the most beautiful of all. He is so young and pretty." And the old swans bowed their heads before him.

Then he hid his head under his wing. He did not know what to do. He was so happy and yet not at all proud. He had been teased and despised for his ugliness, and now he heard them say he was the most beautiful of all the birds. Even the elder tree bent down its branches into the water before him, and the sun shone warm and bright. He rustled his feathers, curved his slender neck, and cried joyfully, from the depths of his heart, "I never dreamed of such happiness as this, while I was an ugly duckling."

THE TRAVELING COMPANION

POOR JOHN was very sad. His father was very ill, and there was no hope of recovery. John sat alone with his father in the little room late into the night.

"You have been a good son, John," whispered his father, "and God will protect and take care of you when I am gone." His father looked at him as he spoke, with mild, earnest eyes. Then he gave a deep sigh and died so quietly that it looked as though he had just fallen asleep.

John wept, for now he had no one in the whole world. No father, no mother, no brother, no sister. Poor John! He knelt down by the bed, kissed his father's hand, and wept for a long time. But at last his eyes closed, and he fell asleep with his head resting against the hard bedpost. While he slept, he had a strange dream. He felt the sun shining on him, and his father was alive and well and laughing. A beautiful girl, with a golden crown on her head and long, shining hair, gave John her hand, and his father said, "What a bride you have won! She is the loveliest maiden on Earth."

Then he awoke, and all the beauty vanished before his eyes. His father lay dead on the bed, and he was all alone. Poor John! The following week his father was buried. John walked behind his dear father's coffin. He heard the earth fall on the coffin lid and watched until only one corner could be seen. At last, that too disappeared. He felt as if his heart would break with the weight of his sorrow. Those who stood around the grave sang a hymn, and the sweet tones brought tears to his eyes again. The sun shone brightly down on the green trees, as if to say, "Don't be so sad, John. Do you see the beautiful blue sky above you? Your father is up there, and he is watching over you."

I will always be good, thought John, and then when I die I will be with my father in heaven. How wonderful it will be to see each other again! How much I shall have to tell him. Oh, what joy it will be! He pictured it all so clearly, that he smiled even while the tears ran down his cheeks.

"*Tweet, tweet!*" The little birds in the chestnut trees twittered happily. It was as if they knew that his father was now in heaven, with wings much larger and more beautiful than their own. John saw them fly away out of the green trees and into the world, and he longed to fly with them. But first he would carve a large wooden cross to place on his father's grave. When he returned with the cross that evening, he found the grave covered with flowers. People who had known his good father had loved him very much.

Early the next morning, John packed up all his money and his little bundle of clothes, for he was determined to try his luck in the world. But first he went into

31

the churchyard. At his father's grave, he offered up a prayer and bid him farewell.

As he passed through the fields, all the flowers looked fresh and beautiful as they nodded in the wind and the warm sunshine. It was as if they were saying, "Welcome to the world where everything is fresh and bright!"

John turned to have one more look at the old church, in which he had been christened as a newborn and where his father had taken him every Sunday to hear the service and join in singing the hymns. As he looked at the old tower, he saw the bell-ringer standing in one of the narrow openings, his little pointed cap on his head, shading his eyes from the sun with one hand. John nodded farewell to him, and the little bell-ringer waved his cap, laid his hand on his heart, and waved good-bye to him.

John continued his journey and thought of all the wonderful things he would see in the big, beautiful world, till he found himself farther away from home than he had ever been before. He did not even know the names of the places he passed through, and he could scarcely understand the language of the people he met, for he was far away, in a strange land. The first night he slept out in the fields on a haystack, for there was no other bed. It seemed so nice and comfortable that even a king would be happy there. The field, the brook, the haystack, and the blue sky formed a beautiful bedroom. The green grass, with the little red and white flowers, was the carpet, the elder bushes and the hedges of wild roses looked like garlands on the walls, and for a bath, he had the clear, fresh water of the brook where the rushes bowed their heads, wishing him good morning and good evening. The moon hung like a large lamp high up in the blue ceiling, and he had no fear of its setting fire to his curtains. John slept there quite safely all night, and when he awoke, the sun was up, and all the little birds were singing round him, "Good morning, good morning. Aren't you up yet?"

It was Sunday, and the bells were ringing for church. As the people went in, John followed them. He heard God's word, joined in singing the hymns, and listened to the preacher. It seemed just like he was in his own church. Out in the churchyard were several graves and, on some of them, the grass had grown very high. John thought of his father's grave that he knew would soon look like these since he was not there to weed and attend to it. Then he set to work, pulled up the high grass, raised the wooden crosses which had fallen down, and replaced the wreaths which had been blown away by the wind, thinking all the time, "Perhaps someone is doing the same for my father's grave, since I am not there to do it."

Outside the church door stood an old beggar, leaning on his crutch. John gave him some coins and continued on his journey, feeling lighter and happier than ever. Toward evening, the weather became very stormy, and he hurried on as quickly as he could to find shelter. But it was quite dark by the time he reached a little lonely church which stood on a hill. "I will go in here," he thought, "and sit down in a corner, for I am very tired and need to rest."

So he went in and sat down. He folded his hands and said his evening prayers. Soon he was fast asleep and dreaming, while outside thunder rolled and lightning flashed. When he awoke, it was still night, but the storm had ended, and the moon shone in upon him through the windows. Then he saw an open coffin standing in the center of the church waiting for burial. John was not at all afraid. He knew that the dead could never hurt anyone. It is the living who harm others. Two such wicked persons stood by the coffin. Their evil intentions were to throw the poor dead body outside the church door and not leave him to rest in his coffin.

"Why would you do this?" asked John, when he heard what they were going to do. "It is very wicked. In the name of Christ, let him rest in peace."

"Nonsense," replied the two dreadful men. "He cheated us. He owed us money which he could not repay, and now he is dead and we shall not get a penny. So we will have our revenge, and let him lie like a dog outside the church door."

"I have only a little money," said John, "it is all I possess in the world, but I will give it to you if you will promise me faithfully to leave this dead man in peace. I shall be able to get on without money. I have strong and healthy limbs, and God will help me."

"Why, of course," said the horrid men, "if you will pay his debt we will both promise not to touch him. You may depend on that." And then they took the money he offered them, laughing at his good nature, and went their way.

When they had left, he laid the man back in the coffin, folded his hands, and went away contentedly through the great forest. All around him he could see the prettiest little elves dancing in the moonlight that shone through the trees. They were not disturbed by his appearance, for they knew he was a good and harmless man. Wicked people would never catch a glimpse of fairies. Some of them were no taller than the width of a finger. They wore golden combs in their long, yellow hair. They were rocking on the large dewdrops that were sprinkled on the leaves and the high

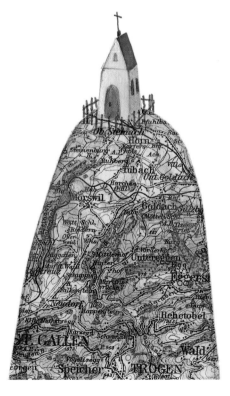

grass. Sometimes the dewdrops would roll away and fall between the stems of the long grass, which caused a great deal of laughing and noise among the little elves. It was quite charming to watch them at play. They sang songs that John remembered singing when he was a little boy.

Large speckled spiders, with silver crowns on their heads, were spinning suspension bridges and palaces from one hedge to another, and when the tiny drops fell upon them, they glittered like shining glass in the moonlight.

This continued till sunrise. Then the little elves crept into the flower buds, and the wind seized the bridges and palaces and blew them into the air like cobwebs. As John left the woods, a man's strong voice called after him, "Hello friend, where are you going?"

"To travel the world," replied John. "I am only a poor lad. I have neither father nor mother, but God will help me."

"I am also traveling the world," replied the stranger. "Shall we keep each other company?"

"Yes, please, join me," said John, and so they went on together. Soon they began to like each other very much, for they were both good; but John soon discovered that the stranger was much wiser than he. He had already traveled all over the world and could describe almost everything.

The sun was high in the sky when they sat down at last to eat their breakfast under a large tree. At that exact moment an old woman walked toward them. She was very old and bent almost in half. She leaned on a walking stick and, on her back, carried a bundle of firewood that she had collected in the forest. She had tied her apron around it, and John saw three large rods and some willow twigs peeking out. Just as she came close to them, her foot slipped and she fell to the ground screaming loudly. The poor old woman had broken her leg! John suggested that they carry the old woman home to her cottage, but the stranger opened his knapsack and took out a box. He said he had a salve that would make her leg well and strong again so that she would be able to walk home herself as if her leg had never been broken. All that he asked for in return were the three rods which she carried in her apron.

"That is too high a price," said the old woman, nodding her head oddly. She did not seem at all inclined to part with the rods. However, it was not very pleasant to lie there with a broken leg either, so finally she gave the rods to him. No sooner had he rubbed her leg with the salve than the old woman stood up and walked even better than before.

"What do you want with those three rods?" John asked his fellow traveler.

"Oh, they will make excellent brooms," he replied. Then they walked on together for a long distance.

"The sky is getting dark," said John. "Look at those thick, heavy clouds."

"Those aren't clouds," replied his fellow traveler. "Those are mountains—tall, lofty mountains—the tops of which are above the clouds. Believe me, it is wonderful to climb so high, and tomorrow we shall be there."

But the mountains were not as close as they appeared, and they had to travel a whole day before they reached them. They passed through black forests and climbed piles of rock as large as a town. The journey had been so tiring that John and his fellow traveler stopped to rest at an inn before continuing on their journey in the morning.

In the large main room of the inn, a great many people had gathered to watch a comedy performed by puppets. The puppeteer had set up his little theater with the spectators sitting around the room. Right in front, in the very best seat, sat a stout butcher, with a large bulldog by his side who seemed ready to bite. He sat staring at everyone else in the room. Then the play began. It was a pretty piece, with a king and a queen who sat on beautiful thrones with golden crowns on their heads. The queen's dress had a very long train. It was a pleasant play, not at all sad.

But just as the queen stood up and walked across the stage, the bulldog, who should have been held back by his master, sprang forward and grabbed the queen in his teeth and snapped her in two. What a disaster! The poor puppeteer was very annoyed and quite sad about his queen. She had been the prettiest puppet he had, and the bulldog had destroyed her.

After the audience had left, John's traveling companion said that he could fix the puppet. He opened his box and rubbed the queen with the same salve which he had used to cure the old woman when she broke her leg. As soon as he was finished, the queen's back became straight again, and she could move her limbs by herself. The puppet could walk and move just like a living creature. The puppeteer was amazed by the puppet who could dance on her own without him pulling any strings. None of the other puppets could do this.

That night, after everyone at the inn had gone to bed, someone sighed deeply and painfully. The sighing continued for a long time. Soon, everyone got up to see what was wrong. The puppeteer went at once to his little theater and found the puppets all lying on the floor sighing piteously and staring with their glass eyes. They wanted to be like the queen and be able to move on their own. The queen threw herself on her knees, took off her beautiful crown, and holding it in her hand, cried, "Take my crown in payment, but please, rub the salve on my husband and his courtiers."

The poor man who owned the theater could hardly refrain from weeping; he was so sorry that he could not help them. He found John's companion and promised him all the money he might earn at the next evening's performance, if he would only rub the salve on four or five of his puppets. But John's fellow traveler said he wanted only the sword which the puppeteer wore at his side. As soon as he received the sword, he rubbed six of the puppets with the salve, and they immediately began to dance so gracefully that all the living people in the room could not help but join in. The coachman danced with the cook, and the waiters with the chambermaids, and all the strangers joined them. Even the tongs and the fire shovel made an attempt, but they fell down after the first jump. So in the end, it was a very merry night.

The next morning John and his companion left the inn to continue their journey through the great pine forests and over the high mountains. They arrived at last at such a great height that towns and villages lay beneath them, and the church steeples looked like little specks between the green trees. They could see for miles round, far away to places they had never visited, and John saw more of the beautiful world than he had ever known existed. The sun shone brightly in the blue sky above, and through the clear mountain air came the sound of a horn, and the soft, sweet notes brought tears to his eyes, and he could not help exclaiming, "How good and loving God is, to give us all this beauty and loveliness in the world!"

His fellow traveler stood by with folded hands, gazing at the dark woods and the towns bathed in the warm sunshine. At that moment, sweet music sounded over their heads. When they looked up, they saw a large white swan hovering in the air, singing. But the song soon became weaker and weaker, the bird's head drooped, and he sank slowly down and lay dead at their feet.

"Such a beautiful bird," said the traveler, "and these large

white wings are wonderful. I will take them with me." So he cut off the wings of the dead swan with one blow and carried them away with him.

They continued their journey over the mountains for many miles, till they reached a large city with hundreds of towers that shone in the sunshine like silver. In the middle of the city stood a splendid marble palace, with a roof of pure red gold, where the king lived. John and his companion did not go into the town immediately, but stopped at an inn outside the town to change their clothes. They wanted to appear respectable as they walked through the streets. The innkeeper told them that the king was a very good man, who never injured any one. But as for his daughter, "Heaven help us!"

She was a wicked princess. She was beautiful—no one was more elegant or prettier than she, but she was a wicked witch. As a result of her actions, many noble young princes had lost their lives. Anyone was free to make her an offer of marriage, were he prince or beggar, it mattered not. She would ask him to guess three questions which she had just thought of, and if he successfully answered them, he would marry her, and be king over all the land when her father died. But if he could not answer these three questions, then she ordered him to be hanged or to have his head cut off. The old king, her father, was very much grieved at her behavior, but he could not stop her from being so wicked, since once he had said she could do as she pleased. Everyone who came and tried the three questions had been unable to answer them and had been hanged or beheaded. They had all been warned ahead of time and should have left her alone. The old king had become so distressed that, for a whole day every year, he and his soldiers knelt and prayed that the princess might change and become good, but she continued to be as wicked as ever.

"What a horrible princess!" said John. "If I were the king, I would have her punished."

Just then they heard people outside shouting, "Hurrah!" Looking out, they saw the princess passing by. She was so beautiful that everybody forgot her wickedness and shouted "Hurrah!" Twelve lovely maidens in white silk dresses, holding golden tulips in their hands, rode by her side on coal-black horses. The princess herself had a snow-white steed, decked with diamonds and rubies. Her dress was gold, and the whip she held in her hand looked like a sunbeam. The golden crown on her head glittered like the stars of heaven and her scarf was formed of thousands of butterflies' wings sewn together.

When John saw her, his face became as red as a drop of blood, and he could scarcely utter a word. The princess looked exactly like the beautiful lady with the golden crown that he had dreamed of the night his father died. She was so lovely that he could not help loving her.

"It cannot be true," he thought, "that she is really a wicked witch, who orders people to be hanged or beheaded if they cannot answer her questions. Everyone has permission to go and ask her hand, even the poorest beggar. I shall pay a visit to the palace," he said. "I must go, for I cannot help myself."

They all advised him not to attempt it, for he would be sure to share the same fate as the rest. His fellow traveler tried to persuade him not to try it, but John seemed quite sure that he would be successful. He brushed his shoes and his coat, washed his face and his hands, combed his soft flaxen hair, and walked to the palace.

"Come in," said the king, as John knocked at the door. John opened it, and the old king, in a robe and embroidered slippers, came toward him. He wore his crown on his head, carried his scepter in one hand, and his orb in the other. "Welcome," he said to John, but when he found that John was another suitor, he began to weep so violently that both the scepter and orb fell to the floor, and he wiped his eyes on his robe.

"Leave her alone," he said. "You will fare as badly as all the others. Come, I will show you." Then he led John out into the

princess' gardens, where he saw a gruesome sight. On every tree hung three or four princes who had wooed the princess, but had not been able to guess the riddles she gave them. Their skeletons rattled in the breeze and so terrified the birds that they dared not venture into the garden. The flowers were supported by human bones instead of sticks, and human skulls were used as flowerpots that grinned horribly. It was really a dreadful garden for a princess. "Do you see all this?" said the old king. "Your fate will be the same as those who are here. Please do not attempt it."

John kissed the good king's hand and said he was sure it would be all right, for he was quite enchanted with the beautiful princess. Then the princess herself came riding into the palace yard with all her ladies. "Good morning," he greeted her. She looked so fair and lovely when she offered her hand to John that he loved her more than ever. How could she be a wicked witch? He accompanied her into the hall where the little pages offered them gingerbread, nuts, and sweetmeats. The old king was so unhappy he could eat nothing. It was decided that John would come to the palace the next day, when the judges and all of the counselors would be present, to try to guess the first riddle. If he succeeded, he would have to come a second time; but if not, he would lose his life—and no one had ever been able to guess even one. However, John was not the least bit anxious. On the contrary, he was very merry. He thought only of the beautiful princess.

When John returned to the inn, he could not refrain from telling his fellow traveler how gracious the princess had been and how beautiful she was. He could hardly wait for the next day. But his friend shook his head and looked very sad. "I do wish you well," he said, "and now I am likely to lose you. Poor dear John! I could cry, but I will not make you unhappy on the last night we may be together. We will be merry, really merry this evening. Tomorrow, after you are gone, I will weep undisturbed."

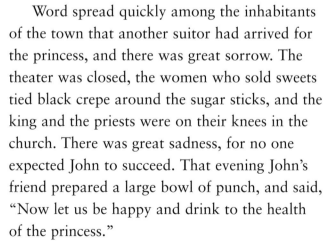

Word spread quickly among the inhabitants of the town that another suitor had arrived for the princess, and there was great sorrow. The theater was closed, the women who sold sweets tied black crepe around the sugar sticks, and the king and the priests were on their knees in the church. There was great sadness, for no one expected John to succeed. That evening John's friend prepared a large bowl of punch, and said, "Now let us be happy and drink to the health of the princess."

But after drinking two glasses, John became so sleepy that he could not keep his eyes open and fell fast asleep. Then his fellow traveler lifted

him gently out of his chair and laid him on the bed. As soon as it was quite dark, he took the two large wings, which he had cut from the dead swan, and tied them firmly to his own shoulders. Then he put the largest of the three rods, which he had gotten from the old woman who had fallen and broken her leg, into his pocket. After this he opened the window and flew over the town, straight toward the palace, where he seated himself in a corner under a window that looked into the bedroom of the princess.

The town was perfectly still when the clocks struck a quarter to twelve. Presently the window opened and the princess, who had large black wings on her shoulders and a long white mantle, flew over the city toward a high mountain.

The fellow traveler, who had made himself invisible so that she could not possibly see him, flew after her through the air and whipped the princess with the rod till she bled whenever he struck her. It was a strange flight through the air! The wind caught her scarf so that it spread out like the sail of a ship and the moon shone through it. "It is hailing so hard!" said the princess, at each blow she received from the rod.

At last she reached the side of the mountain and knocked. The mountain opened with a noise like thunder and the princess went in. The traveler followed her. No one could see him since he had made himself invisible. They went down a long, wide passage. A thousand gleaming spiders ran here and there on the walls, glittering as if they were lit by fire. Next they entered a large hall of silver and gold. Red and blue flowers the size of sunflowers shone on the walls, but no one would dare pick them for their stems were hideous poisonous snakes, and the flowers were flames of fire, darting out of their jaws. Shining glowworms covered the ceiling and sky-blue bats flapped their transparent wings. Altogether the place had a frightful appearance. In the middle of the room stood a throne supported by four skeleton horses whose harnesses were made of fiery-red spiders. The throne itself was made of milk-white glass, and the cushions were little black mice, each biting the other's tail. Over it hung a canopy of rose-colored spiderwebs, spotted with the prettiest little green flies that sparkled like precious stones. On the throne sat an old magician with a crown on his ugly head and a scepter in his hand. He kissed the princess on the forehead, and seated her by his side on the splendid throne. Then the music commenced. Great black grasshoppers played and an owl struck her body like a drum. It was a ridiculous concert. Little black goblins with lights on their caps danced about the hall, but no one could see the traveler. He had placed himself just behind the throne where he could see and hear everything. The courtiers who came in afterward looked noble and grand; but anyone with common sense could see that they were really only broomsticks with cabbages for heads. The magician had given them life and dressed them in embroidered robes.

After there had been a little dancing, the princess told the magician that she had

a new suitor, and asked him what she could think of for the suitor to guess when he came to the castle the next morning.

"Listen to what I say," said the magician, "you must choose something very easy. He is less likely to guess it then. Think of one of your shoes—he will never imagine it is that. Then cut off his head and mind you, do not forget to bring his eyes with you tomorrow night, so I may eat them."

The princess curtsied and said she would not forget the eyes. Then the magician opened the mountain and she flew home again. The traveler followed and beat her so much with the rod that she sighed quite deeply about the heavy hailstorm and went as fast as she could back to her bedroom.

The traveler then returned to the inn where John still slept, took off his wings, and lay down on the bed, for he was very tired. Early in the morning John awoke. When his fellow traveler got up, he told John that he had had a wonderful dream about the princess and her shoe, and he advised John to ask her if she had not thought of her shoe.

"I may as well say that as anything," said John. "Now I will say farewell, for if I guess wrong I shall never see you again."

They embraced and John went into town and walked to the palace. The great hall was full of people. The judges sat in armchairs, with eiderdown cushions to rest their heads upon because they had so much to think of. The old king stood nearby, wiping his eyes with his white handkerchief. When the princess entered, she looked even more beautiful than she had appeared the day before and greeted everyone present most gracefully, but to John she gave her hand and said, "Good morning to you."

Now came the time for John to guess what she was thinking of, and oh, how kindly she looked at him as she spoke. But when he uttered the single word shoe, she turned as pale as a ghost. All her wisdom could not help her, for he had guessed correctly. Oh, how pleased the king was! It was quite amusing to see how he danced about. All the people clapped their hands. His fellow traveler was glad when he heard how successful John had been. But John folded his hands and thanked God, who, he felt quite sure, would help him again as he knew he had to guess twice more.

The evening passed as pleasantly as the preceding one. While John slept, his companion flew behind the princess to the mountain, and beat her even harder than before. This time he had taken two rods with him. No one saw him go in with her and he heard all that was said. This time, the princess was to think of a glove. Again he told John that he had heard it in a dream. The next day, John was once again able to guess correctly, and it caused great rejoicing at the palace. The whole court jumped about as they had seen the king do the day before, but the princess

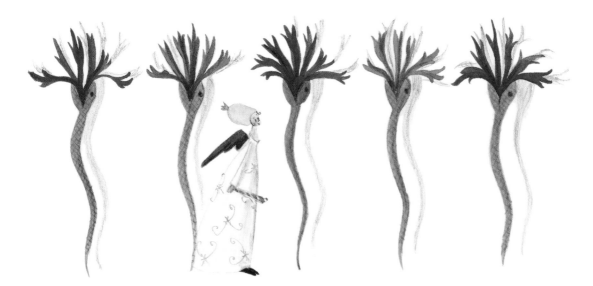

lay on the sofa and would not say a single word. All now depended on John. If he could just guess correctly the third time, he would marry the princess and reign over the kingdom after the death of the old king. But if he failed, he would lose his life and the magician would have his beautiful blue eyes.

That evening, John said his prayers and went to bed very early and soon fell asleep. But his companion tied on his wings, took three rods, and with his sword at his side, flew to the palace. It was a very dark night and so stormy that tiles flew from the roofs of the houses and trees bent themselves like reeds before the wind. Lightning flashed and thunder rolled in one long peal all night. The window of the castle opened and the princess flew out. She was pale as death, but she laughed at the storm as if it were nothing. Her white scarf fluttered in the wind like a sail and the traveler beat her with the three rods till the blood trickled down. At last she could scarcely fly, but she managed to reach the mountain. "What a storm!" she said as she entered. "I have never been out in such awful weather."

Then the princess told the magician that John had guessed correctly a second time, and if he succeeded the next morning, he would win, and she could never come to the mountain again or practice magic as she had done. She was quite unhappy. "I will find something for you to think of which he will never guess, unless he is a greater conjuror than myself. But for now let us be merry."

Then he took the princess by both hands and they danced with all the little goblins and jack-o'-lanterns in the room. The red spiders sprang here and there quite merrily on the walls and the flowers of fire appeared as if they were throwing out sparks. The owl beat her drum, the crickets whistled, and the grasshoppers played.

It was a ridiculous ball. After they had danced enough, the princess was obliged to go home, for fear she should be missed at the palace. The magician offered to go with her to keep her company. They flew away through the bad weather, and the traveler followed them.

He beat them so hard that he broke all three rods across their shoulders. The magician had never been out in such a storm as this. Near the palace, the magician stopped to wish the princess farewell and to whisper in her ear, "Tomorrow think of my head."

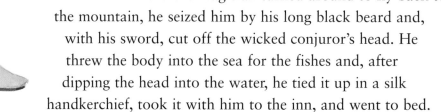

But the traveler heard it, and, just as the princess slipped through the window into her bedroom and the magician turned around to fly back to the mountain, he seized him by his long black beard and, with his sword, cut off the wicked conjuror's head. He threw the body into the sea for the fishes and, after dipping the head into the water, he tied it up in a silk handkerchief, took it with him to the inn, and went to bed.

The next morning he gave John the handkerchief and told him not to untie it till the princess asked him what she was thinking of. There were so many people in the great hall of the palace that they stood as thick as radishes tied together in a bunch. The council sat in their armchairs with the white cushions. The old king wore new robes and the golden crown and scepter had been polished so that he looked quite smart. But the princess was very pale and wore a black dress as if she were going to a funeral.

"What am I thinking of?" asked the princess. John immediately untied the handkerchief and was himself quite frightened when he saw the head of the ugly magician. Everyone shuddered, for it was terrible to see. But the princess sat like a statue and could not utter a single word. At length she rose and gave John her hand, for he had guessed correctly.

She looked at no one, but sighed deeply, and said, "This evening our marriage must take place."

"I am very pleased to hear it," said the old king. "It is just what I wish."

Then all the people shouted "Hurrah!" The band played music in the streets, the bells rang, and the women took the black crepe off the sugar sticks. There was

universal joy. Three oxen, stuffed with ducks and chickens, were roasted whole in the marketplace for everyone to eat. The fountains were filled with the most delicious wine, and whoever bought a penny loaf at the baker's received six large buns full of raisins, as a present. In the evening the whole town was illuminated. The soldiers fired the cannons and the children shot off firecrackers.

There was eating and drinking, dancing and jumping everywhere. In the palace, the highborn gentlemen and beautiful ladies danced with each other, and they could be heard at a great distance singing the following song:

Here are maidens, young and fair,
Dancing in the summer air;
Like two spinning-wheels at play,
Pretty maidens dance away—
Dance the spring and summer through
Till the sole falls from your shoe.

But the princess was still a witch, and she did not love John. His fellow traveler had thought of that, so he gave John three feathers out of the swan's wings and a little bottle with a few drops in it. He told him to put a large bath full of water by the princess's bed and to put the feathers and the drops into it. Then, at the moment she was about to get into bed, he must give her a little push so that she would fall into the water. Then he should dunk her under three times. This would destroy the power of the magician and she would love him very much. John did all that his companion told him to do.

The princess shrieked aloud when he dipped her under the water the first time, and she assumed the form of a great black swan with fiery eyes. As she rose the second time from the water, the swan had become white with a black ring round its neck. John allowed the water to close once more over the bird and at the same time it changed back into a most beautiful princess. She was even lovelier than before, and she thanked him while her eyes sparkled with tears, for he had broken the spell of the magician. The next day, the king came with the whole court to offer their congratulations and stayed quite late. Last of all came John's traveling companion. He had his staff in his hand and his knapsack on his back. John kissed him many times and told him he must not go, he must remain with him, for he was the cause of all his good fortune. But the traveler shook his head, and said gently, "No, my

47

time is up now. I have paid my debt to you. Do you remember the dead man that the bad people wished to throw out of his coffin? You gave all you possessed that he might rest peacefully in his grave. I am that man." As he said this, he vanished.

The wedding festivities lasted a whole month. John and his princess loved each other dearly, and the old king lived to see many a happy day when he took their little children on his knees and let them play with his scepter. And John became king over the whole country.

THERE IS NO DOUBT

"WHAT a terrible affair!" said a hen. "That was a horrible thing to happen in a henhouse. I cannot sleep alone tonight. It is a good thing that so many of us share this roost." And then she told a story that made the feathers on the other hens bristle and the rooster's comb fall down. But there was no doubt about it, and it is perfectly true!

We will begin at the beginning, in a henhouse in another part of town. The sun was setting and the chickens were flying to their perches for the night. Among them was a hen with white feathers and short legs, who, as a hen, was respectable in every way. As she was flying up to the roost, she plucked at herself with her beak and a little feather came out. She watched as it fell to the floor of the henhouse.

"There it goes," she said. "The more I pluck, the more beautiful I become." She said it purely in fun, for she was the best of the hens and, as has already been said, very respectable. With that she went to sleep.

It was dark in the henhouse and hen sat close to hen, but the one who sat nearest to her did not fall asleep right away. She had heard and yet not heard, as we sometimes do in this world, and had missed the merry note of humor in her neighbor's voice. She turned to the chicken on her other side and said, "Did you hear what she just said? I won't mention names, but there is a hen here who intends to pluck herself in order to look beautiful. If I were a rooster, I would despise her."

Just above the chickens sat the owls. The owl family had sharp ears, and they all heard every word. They rolled their eyes, and mother owl, beating her wings, said, "Don't listen to her! But I suppose you heard what was said? I heard it with my own ears, and one has to hear a great deal sometimes before the chickens fall asleep at night. There is one among them who has forgotten what is becoming to a hen and she intends to pluck out all her feathers and let the rooster see it."

"Quiet!" said father owl. "Children should not hear such things."

"But I must tell our neighbor owl about it. She is such a pleasant owl to talk to." And with that she flew away.

"*Who-whoo! Whoo-whoo!*" They both hooted in the neighbor's dovecote to the doves inside. "Have you heard? Have you heard? *Too-whoo!* There is a hen who has plucked out all her feathers for the sake of the rooster. She will freeze to death, if she is not frozen already. *Whoo-whoo!*"

"Where? Where?" cooed the doves.

"In the neighbor's yard. I've practically seen it myself. It is almost unbecoming to tell the story, but there is no doubt about it."

"Believe every word of what we tell you," said the doves as they told the story to the other doves. "There is a hen—some say that there are two—who has plucked out all her feathers in order not to look like the others and to attract the attention of the rooster. It is a dangerous game, for one can easily catch cold and die from fever, and she's already dead."

"Wake up! Wake up!" crowed the rooster who had overheard the doves. Sleep was still in his eyes, but he crowed out: "Three hens have died of their unfortunate love for a rooster. They plucked out all their feathers. It is a horrible story, and I can not keep it to myself. Quick, tell the others!"

"Quick, tell everyone!" shrieked the bats, and the hens clucked and the roosters crowed, "Tell everyone, tell them all!" In this way the story traveled from yard to yard, until at last it came back to the place where it had started.

"Five hens," it now ran, "have plucked out all their feathers to show which of them had grown leanest for love of the rooster, and then they all pecked at each other till the blood ran down and they fell down dead."

The hen who had lost the already loose little feather naturally did not recognize her own story and, being a respectable hen, said, "I despise those chickens. But there are always a few bad hens in every roost. Such things shouldn't be concealed, and I will do my best to get the story into the papers so that it becomes known throughout the land."

It got into the papers, it was printed, and there is no doubt—it is perfectly true, that one little feather can easily grow into five hens.

THE LITTLE MATCH GIRL

IT WAS bitterly cold. Snow was falling, and it was beginning to get dark. This was
the last evening of the year, New Year's Eve. A poor little girl was walking through
the streets in the cold and the dark. Her head and feet were bare. She had been
wearing slippers when she left home, but that did her no good now! They had been
far too big for her—they were really her mother's slippers, and they were so big that
they came off as the little girl hurried over the road to get out of the way of two
carriages driving along at high speed. When the carriages had passed, she couldn't
find one of the slippers at all, and a boy ran off with the other, saying he would use
it for a cradle when he had a child himself.

So now the little girl was walking along with nothing on her feet, which were
red and blue with cold. She had some matches in her apron, and she was holding
another bundle of matches, but no one had bought any from her all day long. No
one had given her a penny. Hungry and chilled to the bone, the poor little thing
went on her way, a picture of misery. The snowflakes fell on her long yellow hair.
It curled nicely on her neck, but she never gave her own pretty looks a thought.
Lights were shining in all the windows, and there was a delicious smell of roast
goose in the streets, for this was New Year's Eve. She did think about that.

She sat down in a corner between two houses, one of them standing out farther
into the street than the other, and curled her little legs up under her, but now she felt
even colder than before. She dared not go home because she had sold no matches,
she hadn't earned a penny, and she was afraid her father would beat her. It was cold
at home too. The place was only an attic and, although the biggest chinks in the
roof were stuffed with straw and rags, the wind still came in. Her little hands were
numb with cold. Perhaps the flame of a match would do them good! Dare she take
one out of the bundle, strike it on the wall, and warm her fingers? She did. She
drew one out, struck it—and oh, how it sparked and burned! It gave a warm, clear
light like a little candle. She cupped her hand around it. What a strange light it was!
The little girl felt as if she were sitting by a big iron stove decorated with shiny
brass balls and bars, with a lovely warm fire burning in it. She stretched out her feet
to get them warm too—but then the flame went out. The iron stove disappeared,
and there she sat with the tiny end of the burned match in her hand.

She struck another match. It burned and shone, and where its light fell the wall
seemed to become transparent, so that she could see into the room inside. There
was a table laid with a spotless white cloth, fine china, and a roast goose stuffed
with prunes and apples, which smelled delicious. Better still, the goose jumped off
its dish, although it had a knife and fork stuck in it, and waddled across the floor

toward the little girl. But then the match went out, and there was nothing to be seen but the hard, cold wall.

She struck a third match, and now she was sitting under a beautiful Christmas tree, much bigger and more handsomely decorated than the one she had seen through the rich merchant's glass doors on Christmas Eve.

A thousand candles were burning on the green branches, and brightly colored figures such as you see in shop windows looked down on her. The little girl reached both hands out in the air— but then the match went out. The flames of all the Christmas candles burned higher and higher, and she saw that they were bright stars. One of them fell, leaving a fiery trail in the sky behind it.

"Someone is dying," said the little girl, for her old grandmother used to say that when a star falls, a soul is going to God. Her grandmother, who was dead now, was the only person who had ever been kind to her.

She struck another match on the wall. It flared up, and in its light she saw her old grandmother, bright, shining, and kind. What a welcome sight that was! "Oh, Grandmother!" called the little girl. "Take me with you! I know you'll go when the match goes out, like the warm stove, the delicious roast goose, and the beautiful big Christmas tree!"

And she hastily struck all the rest of the matches in her bundle to keep her grandmother there. The matches burned with such light it was brighter than day. Her grandmother had never looked so tall and beautiful before. She picked the little girl up in her arms, and they flew away in joy and glory, up and up, going to the place where there is no cold or hunger or pain anymore, going to be with God.

The little girl was found in the corner between two houses in the cold light of dawn. Her cheeks were red and there was a smile on her lips, but she was dead, frozen to death on the last evening of the old year.

The sun of New Year's Day rose over the little body, sitting there with the bundle of burned matches.

"Trying to keep warm," they said. No one knew what beautiful visions she had seen or how she and her old grandmother had gone away into the glory and joy of the New Year.

THE SWINEHERD

ONCE UPON A TIME, there was a prince, and he was poor. He had a kingdom—but only a little one. Still, it was big enough for him to dream of marrying, which is what he wanted to do. He was aiming rather high in daring to ask for the hand of the emperor's daughter. And, since his name was known far and wide, and there were hundreds of princesses who would have said yes, that is what he did. But what did the emperor's daughter say? Well, we shall see!

There was a rose tree growing on the grave of the prince's father, and what a beautiful rose tree it was. It flowered only once every five years, and then it bore only one rose, but that rose had so sweet a fragrance that anyone who smelled it forgot all his cares and sorrows. And the prince also had a nightingale that could sing as if its little throat held all the lovely music in the world. He thought he would give the rose and the nightingale to the princess, so they were put into large silver vessels and sent to her. The emperor had the vessels brought before him in the great hall, where the princess and her ladies-in-waiting were playing "Going Visiting." That was all they ever did with their time. When the princess saw the big vessels holding her presents, she clapped her hands for joy.

"I hope there's a little cat inside!" she said. However, what she found was the lovely rose.

"Isn't it nicely made!" said the ladies-in-waiting.

"Nicely?" said the emperor. "It's better than nice, it is beautiful!" But when the princess touched the rose, she could have wept.

"Oh dear, Papa!" she said. "It isn't artificial after all, it's *real!*"

"Oh dear!" said all the courtiers. "It's real!"

"Well, let's see what's in the other vessel before we lose our tempers," said the emperor. Out came the nightingale. It sang so sweetly that at first they could not say a word against it.

"*Superbe! Charmante!*" remarked the ladies-in-waiting, who all spoke French, and spoke it very badly.

"That bird reminds me of the late empress' music box!" said one old courtier. "The notes and the way it sings are just the same."

"So they are," said the emperor, and wept like a little child.

"You can't tell me *that's* real!" said the princess.

"Oh yes, it's a real bird sure enough," said the man who had brought it.

"Then it can fly away!" said the princess, and nothing would persuade her to let the prince come and see her.

But he was not going to lose heart; he smeared his face with dirt, leaving black and brown marks, jammed his hat down on his head, and knocked on the emperor's door. "Good day, Emperor!" said he. "May I have a job at the palace?"

"Dear me, there are so many people who want to work here!" said the Emperor. "However, let's see—I do need someone to look after the pigs. We have a great many pigs."

So the prince was made the court swineherd. He was given a miserable little room near the pigsty, and there he had to stay. He sat and worked all day, and by the time evening came, he had made a nice little pan with bells all around it. Whenever the pan came to a boil, the bells rang out very prettily, playing the old tune:

Oh, my dearest Augustine,
All's lost, lost, lost!

However, the most remarkable thing of all was that when you held your finger in the steam coming from the pan, you could immediately smell what was being cooked on every hearth in town. That was certainly a far cry from the rose!

Along came the princess with all her ladies-in-waiting, and she heard the tune. She stopped and looked pleased; the fact was, she could play "Oh, my dearest Augustine" herself. Indeed, it was the *only* tune she could play, and she played it with one finger at that.

"That's my own tune!" she said. "What a well-educated swineherd he must be! Go in and ask him what his musical instrument costs."

So one of the ladies-in-waiting went in, putting clogs on first. "What do you want for that pan?" asked the lady-in-waiting.

"Ten kisses from the princess," said the swineherd.

"Mercy on us!" said the lady.

"I can't take less," said the swineherd.

"Well," asked the princess, "what did he say?"

"Oh dear," said the lady-in-waiting, "I really can't bring myself to tell you, it's so shocking!"

"Then whisper it!" So the lady whispered.

"Good gracious, how rude of him!" said the princess, and she walked away. But she had not gone far before the bells rang out with their pretty tune again:

Oh, my dearest Augustine,
All's lost, lost, lost!

"Go and ask him if he'll take ten kisses from my ladies instead," said the princess.

"No, thank you," said the swineherd. "Ten kisses from the princess, or I keep my pan."

"The impertinence of it!" said the princess. "Oh well, you must all stand in front of me so nobody can see."

So the ladies-in-waiting stood in front of her and held out the skirts of their dresses, and the swineherd got his ten kisses and the princess got the pan. What fun the princess and her ladies had! They made the pan boil all evening and all next day, and they knew what was cooking on every fire in town, from the lord chamberlain's to the cobbler's. The ladies-in-waiting danced about, clapping their hands.

"We know who's having sweet soup and who's having pancakes! We know who's having porridge and who's having cutlets! Isn't that interesting?"

"Very interesting indeed," said the mistress of the royal household.

"But you must keep it secret," said the princess, "because I'm the emperor's daughter!"

"Of course we will," everyone said.

The swineherd, who was really a prince—though they didn't know it—did not sit idle all day. He made a rattle. When you swung the rattle around, it played all the waltzes and jigs and polkas that have ever been heard since the world began.

"How delightful!" said the princess as she walked by. "I never heard a better tune! Go in and ask him what that instrument costs—and mind you I'm not kissing him again!"

"He wants a hundred kisses from the princess," said the lady who had gone to ask.

"He must be crazy!" said the princess, and she walked away, but before she had gone far she stopped. "Well, one must encourage art," said she, "and I *am* the emperor's daughter! Tell him I'll give him ten kisses, the same as yesterday, and he can have the rest from my ladies."

"Oh," said the ladies, "we wouldn't like that."

"Nonsense!" said the princess. "If I can kiss him, so can you. Don't forget I pay your wages!"

So the lady-in-waiting had to go and see the swineherd again.

"A hundred kisses from the princess herself," he said, "or we each keep what's our own."

"Stand in front of me," said the princess, so all the ladies-in-waiting stood in front of her, and she and the swineherd started kissing.

"What's that crowd doing down by the pigsty?" asked

the emperor, who had gone out onto his balcony. He rubbed his eyes and put his spectacles on. "Oh, it's the ladies-in-waiting playing some kind of game. I'll go and see what they're up to!" And he pulled on his slippers, which were trodden at the heel. He was in a great hurry! As soon as he was down in the courtyard, he went along very quietly. The ladies-in-waiting were so busy counting kisses to make sure it was all fair and the swineherd did not get too many or too few, they never noticed the emperor. He stood on tiptoe.

"What's all this?" said he, seeing the kissing, and he hit them over the head with his slipper, just as the swineherd was taking his eighty-sixth kiss. "Get out!" said the emperor furiously, and the princess and the swineherd were both turned out of his empire. So there stood the princess, crying, and the swineherd was angry, and the rain poured down.

"Poor me! I'm so miserable!" said the princess. "If only I'd taken that handsome prince! Oh, how unhappy I am!"

Then the swineherd went behind a tree, wiped the black and brown smears off his face, cast his dirty clothes aside, and came back in his royal robes, looking so fine that the princess bowed down to him.

"Now that I know you, I despise you!" he said. "You wouldn't marry an honest prince, you didn't know the true value of the rose and the nightingale, but you were ready to kiss the swineherd just for a toy! It serves you right."

And he went home to his own kingdom and shut and locked the door. All she could do was stand outside and sing:

Oh, my dearest Augustine,
All's lost, lost, lost!

THUMBELINE

ONCE UPON A TIME, there was a woman who longed to have a tiny child of her own, but she had no idea where to get one. So she went to see an old witch and asked her, "I do so long to have a little child. Won't you tell me where I can get one?"

"Oh, we'll soon deal with that," said the witch. "Here, take this barleycorn. It is no ordinary barleycorn, not the kind that grows in farmers' fields or is given to the chickens to eat! Put it in a flowerpot, and you will see what you will see!"

"Thank you kindly," said the woman, and she gave the witch some money. Then she went home and planted the barleycorn, and it instantly grew into a large and beautiful flower. The flower looked just like a tulip, but its petals were slightly curled as if it were still in bud.

"What a lovely flower!" said the woman, and she kissed its beautiful red-and-yellow petals. The moment that she kissed it, the flower burst open with a loud snap. Now it really looked like a tulip, but in its green center sat a tiny little girl, very delicate and sweet. She was no bigger than your thumb, and so she was called Thumbeline.

She was given a prettily lacquered walnut shell for a cradle, and she lay there on blue violet petals with a rose petal coverlet over her. She slept in her cradle by night, and by day she played on a table. The woman had put a plate on the table, holding a wreath of flowers with their stalks hanging down in the water and a big tulip petal floating on top of it. Thumbeline could ferry herself from one side of the plate to the other on this petal, using two white horsehairs for oars. It was a pretty sight. She could sing too, in the sweetest, loveliest voice that ever was heard.

One night as she lay in her pretty little bed, an ugly toad came hopping in through the window, which had a broken pane. The toad was big and ugly and wet. She hopped right over to the table where Thumbeline lay asleep under her red rose petal. "What a nice wife she would make for my son!" said the toad. And she picked up the walnut shell where Thumbeline lay asleep and hopped away with it, right through the broken pane and out into the garden.

There was a big, broad stream running by the house. Its banks were all muddy

and marshy, and the toad lived here with her son. Oh dear, he was so ugly and nasty. He looked just like his mother!

All he could say when he saw the sweet little girl in her walnut shell was, *"Croak! Croak! Croak, croak, croak!"*

"Don't speak so loudly, or you'll wake her," said the old mother toad. "She could still run away from us, for she's as light as swans' down. We will place her on one of the big water-lily leaves on the stream. Little and light as she is, it will be like an island to her! She won't be able to run away from us while we clear out our best room down in the mud, where the pair of you are to keep house."

There were a great many water lilies growing out in the stream, with broad green leaves that looked as if they were floating on top of the water. The leaf that was farthest away was the biggest one, too. The old mother toad swam out to this leaf and placed Thumbeline in her walnut shell on it.

The poor little thing woke up very early the next morning, and when she saw where she was, she began to weep bitterly, for there was water all around the big green leaf and she could not get to land at all.

The old toad was down in the mud, decking out her best room with reeds and yellow marsh marigold petals to make it pretty for her new daughter-in-law. Then she and her ugly son swam out to the leaf where Thumbeline lay. They were going to fetch her pretty bed and put it in the bridal chamber before Thumbeline arrived. The old mother toad curtsied low in the water and said, "This is my son, who is to be your husband, and the two of you will live very comfortably together down in the mud!"

"Croak! Croak! Croak, croak, croak!" was all her son could find to say.

Then she picked up the little bed and swam away with it. Thumbeline sat all alone on the green leaf, weeping because she did not want to live with the nasty toad or be married to her ugly son. The little fish swimming down in the water must have seen the toad and heard what she said, for they put their heads out to see the little girl for themselves. As soon as they set eyes on her, they loved her so much that they would have been very sorry to see her forced to go down and live with the ugly toad! No, that must never be! They clustered together in the water around the green stalk of the leaf on which she was sitting and nibbled through it with their teeth. Then the leaf with Thumbeline floated downstream far, far away, where the toad could not follow. Thumbeline floated past a great many places, and the little birds perching in the bushes saw her and sang, "Oh, what a lovely little lady!" The leaf floated on and on with her, and so Thumbeline came to another country.

A little white butterfly kept flying around Thumbeline and at last settled on the leaf, for it had taken a liking to the little girl. Thumbeline was very happy now. The toads could no longer get at her, and they were passing such pretty scenery.

The sun shone on the water like glimmering gold, and as the leaf sped along even faster, Thumbeline took her sash and tied one end to the butterfly and the other to the leaf.

At that moment, a big June beetle came flying up and saw her. He immediately clasped her slender waist with his claws and flew up into a tree with her.

But the green leaf floated on downstream, taking the butterfly with it, for the butterfly was tied to the leaf and could not get away.

Oh dear, how frightened poor Thumbeline was when the June beetle flew up into the tree with her. She was saddest of all because of the pretty white butterfly she had tied to the leaf. If it could not get free, it would starve to death! But the June beetle didn't care about that. He settled on the biggest green leaf in the tree, gave her nectar from the flowers to eat, and said she was very pretty, even if she was not in the least like a June beetle. Then all the other June beetles who lived in that tree came visiting. They looked at Thumbeline, and the June beetle girls shrugged their feelers and said, "Why, she has only two legs—what a wretched sight!"

"Oh, she has no feelers!" they said. "And her waist is so slim! She looks just like a human being. How ugly she is!" Yet Thumbeline was very pretty indeed. Or so thought the June beetle who had caught her. But when all the others said she was ugly, he ended up believing them and did not want her anymore, so now she could go where she liked. They flew down from the tree with her and put her on a daisy.

She cried, because she was so ugly that the June beetles didn't want anything to do with her—and yet she was the prettiest thing you ever saw, as fine and bright as the loveliest of rose petals.

All summer long poor Thumbeline lived alone in the great wood. She wove herself a bed of grass blades and slung it under a big burdock leaf, so that the rain could not get at her; she squeezed nectar from the flowers and ate it; and she drank the dew that stood on the leaves every morning. So summer and autumn passed by, but then winter came, and the winter was long and cold. All the birds who had sung so beautifully for her flew away. The trees and the flowers faded, the big burdock leaf under which she had slept curled up and became a yellow, withered stem, and she was terribly cold, for her clothes were worn out. Poor little Thumbeline was so tiny and delicate that she was in danger of freezing to death. It began to snow, and every snowflake that fell on her was like a whole shovelful being thrown on one of us, since we are big folk, and she was only the size of your thumb. So she wrapped herself in a dead leaf, but there was no warmth in it, and she shivered with the cold. Beyond the wood to which she had come there lay a big wheat field, but the wheat had been cut long ago, and there was only bare, dry stubble on the frozen ground. The stubble was like a forest to Thumbeline as she walked through it, trembling dreadfully with cold. At last she came to a field mouse's door, a little hole down among the stubble. The field mouse was very warm and comfortable living down there, with a whole room full of grain and a fine kitchen and a larder. Poor Thumbeline stood at her door like a beggar girl, asking for a tiny piece of barleycorn, because she had had nothing at all to eat for two days.

"You poor little thing!" said the field mouse, who was a good old creature at heart. "Come into my nice warm room and share my meal!" She took a fancy to Thumbeline and told her, "You can stay the winter with me if you like, but you must keep my house clean and tell me stories. I'm very fond of stories." So Thumbeline did as the good old field mouse asked, and she was very comfortable indeed.

"We'll soon be having a visitor," said the field mouse. "My neighbor usually comes to visit me every day of the week. He is even better off than I am, and has a finer house, with great big rooms to live in, and he wears a fine black velvet fur coat. If you could only marry him, you'd be well provided for. But he can't see, so you must tell him the very best stories you know!"

However, Thumbeline did not like this idea. She didn't want to marry the neighbor one bit, for he was a mole.

And so he came visiting in his black velvet coat. The field mouse said he was very rich and very clever, and his property was over twenty times bigger than hers. The mole knew all sorts of things, but he could not bear the sun and the pretty flowers, and he never spoke well of them because he had never seen them. Thumbeline had

65

to sing for him, so she sang "Ladybird, ladybird, fly away home," and "The monk in the meadow." The mole fell in love with her for her pretty voice, but he said nothing yet, for he was a very cautious man.

Recently he had dug a long passage through the earth from his house to the field mouse's, and he said the field mouse and Thumbeline could walk there whenever they liked. He told them not to be afraid of the dead bird lying in the passage. The bird was a whole one, with beak and feathers and all. It must have just died when winter came, and now it lay buried on the spot where he had dug his own passage.

The mole took a piece of rotten wood in his mouth, for rotten wood shines like fire in the dark, and went ahead to light the way down the long, dark passage for them. When they came to the place where the dead bird lay, the mole put his big nose against the roof and pushed up the earth, making a large hole so that the light could shine in. In the middle of the floor lay a dead swallow, its beautiful wings close to its sides, its legs and head tucked into its feathers. Poor bird, it must surely have died of cold. Thumbeline felt very sorry for it, for she loved all the little birds dearly. They had sung and chirped for her so prettily all summer long. But the mole gave it a kick with his stumpy leg and said, "That's the end of all his twittering! How miserable to be born a bird! Thank heaven none of my own children will be birds—all a bird can do is sing and then starve to death in the winter."

"You are a sensible man, and you may well say so," agreed the field mouse.

"What reward does a bird get for its singing when winter comes? It must starve and freeze, and yet birds are thought so wonderful!"

Thumbeline said nothing, but when the other two had turned their backs on the bird she bent down, parted the feathers over its head, and kissed its closed eyes.

Perhaps this was the very bird that sang so beautifully for me in the summer, she thought. How happy the dear, pretty bird made me then!

The mole stopped up the hole through which daylight shone in and took the ladies home again. That night, however, Thumbeline could not sleep. She made a beautiful big blanket out of hay, carried it down, and wrapped it around the pretty bird. She tucked some soft cotton she had found in the field mouse's house close to the bird's sides, to make him a warm place to lie in the cold earth.

"Good-bye, you lovely little bird!" she said. "Good-bye and thank you for your beautiful songs in the summer, when all the trees were green and the sun shone so warmly!" And she laid her head on the bird's breast. Then she had a shock, for it felt as if something were beating inside. It was the bird's heart! The swallow was not dead, only unconscious, and now that he was warmer, he was coming back to life. Swallows all fly to the warm countries in autumn, but if one of them lingers too long it freezes, falls to the ground, and lies where it has fallen as if dead, and the cold snow covers it up.

Thumbeline was trembling with fright, for as she was only the size of your thumb, the bird looked gigantic to her. But she plucked up her courage, tucked the cotton closer around the poor swallow, and fetched a mint leaf she herself had been using as a coverlet to lay over the bird's head.

The next night she slipped down to see him again. He was awake, but so tired he could only open his eyes for a moment, to see Thumbeline standing there with a piece of rotten wood in her hand, since she had no other lantern.

"Thank you, my dear sweet child, thank you!" said the sick swallow. "I am so nice and warm now! I'll soon have my strength back, and then I'll be able to fly out into the warm sunshine again!"

"Oh, but it's so cold outside now!" she said. "It is snowing and freezing! You must stay warm in bed, and I'll look after you!"

She brought the swallow water in a flower petal. He drank it and told her he had hurt a wing on a thornbush, so that he could not fly as fast as the other swallows when they all went far, far away to the warm countries. At last he had fallen to the ground, and that was all he knew. He had no idea how he had come to be under the ground.

So he stayed down there all winter, and Thumbeline was good to him and loved him very much. She did not let the mole or the field mouse know anything about it, because they would not care about helping the poor sick swallow.

As soon as spring came, and the sun's rays warmed the earth, the swallow said good-bye to Thumbeline. She opened up the hole the mole had made in the roof overhead. The sun shone in on them so beautifully, and the swallow asked if she would like to come with him. He said she could sit on his back, and they would fly far away into the green wood. But Thumbeline knew it would hurt the old field mouse's feelings if she left like that.

"No," said Thumbeline, "I can't go."

"Good-bye, good-bye, you sweet, good girl," said the swallow, and he flew out into the sunshine. Thumbeline watched him go, and tears came to her eyes, because she loved the poor swallow so much.

"*Tweet! Tweet!*" sang the bird, and he flew away into the green wood.

Thumbeline was very sad. She was not allowed to go out into the warm sunlight. The seed corn sown in the field above the mouse's hole was growing tall now, and it was like a thick forest to a poor little girl only as big as your thumb.

"You must spend the summer sewing your trousseau!" the field mouse told her, for neighbor mole, who was so tedious but had a black velvet fur coat, had asked for her hand in marriage. "When you are married to the mole, you will have both woolen underclothes and household linens."

So Thumbeline had to sit at the distaff and spin, and the field mouse hired four spiders to come too, and spin and weave by day and by night. Every evening the mole came visiting, and he always said that when the summer came to an end and the sun was not as hot as it was now, when it baked the earth as hard as stone—yes, when summer was over, his wedding to Thumbeline would be held. She did not like the thought of it at all, for she could not bear the tedious mole. Every morning at sunrise, and every evening at sunset, she would slip outside the door, and when the wind blew the ears of wheat apart so that she could see the blue sky, she thought how bright and lovely it was out here, and longed to see her old friend the swallow again. But the swallow did not come back. He had flown far away into the beautiful green wood.

When autumn came Thumbeline had her trousseau ready. "You are to be married in four weeks' time," the field mouse told her.

But Thumbeline wept and said she did not want to marry the tiresome old mole. "Fiddle-de-dee!" said the field mouse. "Don't be so stubborn, or I'll bite you with my white teeth! It's a very fine husband you are getting! Why, the queen herself does not own a black velvet fur coat the likes of his. He has stores in his kitchen and his cellar, and you ought to thank heaven for him!"

So the wedding was to take place. The mole had already come to fetch Thumbeline away to live with him deep down underground. They would never again come out to see the warm sun, for the mole could not stand sunshine. Poor child, she was very unhappy to have to say good-bye to the beautiful sun. While she was living with the field mouse she had at least been able to step outside the door and see it.

"Good-bye, bright sun!" she said, stretching her arms up into the air, and she walked a little way beyond the field mouse's hole, for the wheat had been reaped now and there was nothing left but dry stubble. "Good-bye, good-bye!" she said,

putting her arms around a little red flower that grew there. "Give my love to my dear swallow, if you see him!"

"*Tweet! Tweet!*" sang a voice overhead at that very moment. She looked up, and it was the swallow flying by. He was delighted to see Thumbeline. She told him how little she liked the thought of marrying the ugly mole and going to live underground where the sun never shone. She had to shed tears—she could not help it.

"The cold winter is coming," said the swallow. "I'm flying away to the warm countries. Would you like to come with me? You can sit on my back. Just tie yourself on with your sash, and we'll fly away from the ugly mole and his dark house, far away over the mountains to the warm countries, where the sun shines more beautifully than it does here, and where it is always summer and there are lovely flowers. Do fly away with me, dear little Thumbeline who saved my life when I lay frozen in the dark underground!"

"Oh yes, I'll come with you!" said Thumbeline, and she sat on the bird's back, with her feet on his outspread wings, and tied her sash to one of his strongest feathers. Then the swallow flew high up into the air, over the woods and over the water, over the high mountains where snow lies all the year round. Thumbeline was freezing in the cold air, but she crept in among the bird's warm feathers and just put her little head out to see all the wonders down below. Soon they came to the warm countries. The sun shone much more brightly there than it does here, the sky was twice as high, and the most beautiful green and blue grapes grew all along the ditches and the hedges. The woods were full of oranges and lemons, the air was fragrant with myrtle and mint, and the prettiest of children ran down the road playing with big, bright butterflies.

But still the swallow flew on, and everything became even more beautiful. A shining white marble castle from olden days stood beneath splendid green trees by the side of a blue lake. Vines clambered around its tall columns, and there were a great many swallows' nests up at the top. One of them belonged to the swallow who was carrying Thumbeline.

"Here is my home," said the swallow. "But if you'd like to choose one of the magnificent flowers growing down below for yourself, I'll put you into it, and you will live there as comfortably as ever you could wish!"

"Oh, that would be wonderful!" she said, clapping her little hands. One big white marble column had fallen to the ground and was broken into three, but the loveliest big white flowers grew among its pieces. The swallow flew down with Thumbeline and put her on the wide petals of one of these flowers. How surprised she was to see a little man sitting in the middle of the flower! He was as pale and clear as if he were made of glass, and he wore the dearest little gold crown on his head, and had the loveliest bright wings on his shoulders. He was the spirit of the

flower, and he himself was no bigger than Thumbeline. There was a little man or woman like him living in every flower, but he was the king of them all.

"Oh, how handsome he is!" Thumbeline whispered to the swallow. As for the little prince, he was quite frightened of the swallow, for the bird was enormous compared to his own small and delicate self. But when he set eyes on Thumbeline he was delighted, for she was the most beautiful girl he had ever seen. So he took the gold crown off his head and put it on hers and asked her name. Then he asked if she would be his wife and become the queen of all the flowers! Well, this was a nicer sort of husband than the toad's son, or the mole with his black velvet fur coat. So she said yes to the handsome prince.

Then a little lady or a little gentleman came out of every flower, all so pretty that it was a joy to see them. They all brought Thumbeline presents, and the best of all was a pair of lovely wings from a big white fly. The wings were fastened to Thumbeline's back, and now she too could fly from flower to flower. How happy they all were! The swallow sat in his nest and sang for them with all his might. But he was sad at heart, for he loved Thumbeline and never wanted to part with her.

"You must not be called Thumbeline anymore," said the prince of flowers. "It's an ugly name, and you are so beautiful. We will call you Maia!"

"Good-bye, good-bye!" said the swallow, for it had come to be the season for him to fly away from the warm countries, far away and back again to Denmark. There he had a little nest above the window where the man who tells fairy tales lives. The swallow sang, *"Tweet, tweet!"* to the man, and that is how we come to know the whole story.

THE SWEETHEARTS

A TOP and a little ball lay together in a box among the other toys. One day, the top said to the ball, "Should we get married? After all, we live in the same box."

But the ball, who was covered in Moroccan leather and thought herself quite refined, did not even reply. The next day, the little boy to whom the playthings belonged painted the top red and yellow and drove a brass-headed nail into its middle, so that while the top was spinning around it looked quite splendid.

"Look at me," said the top to the ball. "What do you say now? Shall we become engaged? We suit each other so well. You spring and I dance. No one would be happier together than the two of us."

"Indeed! Do you think so? Perhaps you are not aware that my father and mother were Moroccan slippers and that I have Spanish cork in my body."

"Yes, but I am made of mahogany," said the top. "A major made me on his lathe."

"Truly?" asked the ball.

"May I never be spun again," said the top, "if I am not telling you the truth."

"You certainly know how to turn a phrase," said the ball, "but I cannot accept your proposal. I am almost engaged to a swallow. Every time I fly up in the air, he puts his head out of the nest and says, 'Will you?' and I have said 'Yes' to myself silently, and that is as good as being almost engaged. But I will promise never to forget you."

"What good is that to me?" asked the top, and they did not speak to each other anymore.

The next day, the boy took the ball outside. The top saw the ball flying high in the air, like a bird, till it went out of sight. Each time it came back and touched Earth, it leapt even higher than before. But the ninth time it rose in the air, it did not return. The boy searched everywhere for it, but it could not be found. It was gone.

"I know very well where she is," sighed the top. "She is in the swallow's nest and has married the swallow." The more the top thought of this, the more he longed for the ball. His love grew even more because he could not have her—that she had been won by another was the worst of all. The top still twirled about and hummed, but he continued to think of the ball. The more he thought of her, the more beautiful she became in his memory. Several years passed, and his love became quite old. The top was no longer young, but he looked more handsome than ever, for someone had painted him with gold paint. He was now a golden top, and he whirled and danced about till he hummed quite loudly. He was something worth looking at. However, one day he leapt too high and disappeared. Everyone searched from the attic to the cellar, but he was nowhere to be found. Where could he be?

He had jumped into the trash bin with all sorts of rubbish. Cabbage stalks, dust, and things that had fallen down from the gutter on the roof were jumbled around him.

This is not a nice place, he thought. My gold paint will soon wear off in here. Oh dear, what a lot of rubbish I have landed in! He noticed a curious round thing that looked a little like an old apple, which lay near a long, leafless cabbage stalk. It was, however, not an apple, but an old ball, which had lain in the gutter for years and become a little swollen and moldy from the rainwater.

"Thank goodness, finally someone of my own class who I can talk to," said the ball, looking at the gilded top. "I am made of Moroccan leather," she said. "I was sewn by a young lady, and I have Spanish cork in my body. I know I might not look like it now. I was once engaged to a swallow, but I fell into the gutter on the roof and I lay there for more than five years. I became thoroughly drenched until finally I rolled out and into this trash bin."

The top said nothing, but he thought of his old love. The more she said, the clearer it became to him that this was the same ball. Just then, the servant came to clean out the trash bin.

"Oh," she exclaimed, picking him up, "here is that gilt top."

So the top was brought inside the house again. Nothing more was heard of the little ball. He spoke not a word about her for his love had died away. After all, when your beloved has lain for five years in a gutter and has been drenched through, love fades on meeting her again in a trash bin.

THE STEADFAST TIN SOLDIER

ONCE UPON A TIME, there were twenty-five tin soldiers who were all brothers, for they had been made from the same tin spoon. They stood straight, with their rifles at their shoulders, in splendid uniforms of red and blue. The very first words they ever heard were, "Tin soldiers!" uttered by a little boy who clapped his hands with delight when he opened the box that contained them. They had been given to him for his birthday, and he stood at the table to set them up. The soldiers were all exactly alike, except for one, who had only one leg. He had been the last one made, and there hadn't been enough of the melted tin to finish him. Instead, he was made so he could stand firmly on one leg, which was rather remarkable.

The table was covered with other playthings, but the most beautiful was a little paper castle. Its rooms could be seen through small windows, and, in front of the castle, little trees surrounded a piece of mirror intended to represent a lake. Swans made of wax swam on the lake, and were reflected in it. All of this was very lovely, but the loveliest of all was a tiny ballerina who stood at the open door of the castle. Like the castle, she was also made of paper. She wore a dress of muslin and over her shoulders a narrow blue ribbon was held in place by a silver rosette almost as large as her face. The little ballerina stood with her arms outstretched and one of her legs raised so high behind her that it disappeared beneath her skirt. The tin soldier could not see it at all and so he thought that she, like himself, had only one leg.

That is the wife for me, he thought, but she is too grand. She lives in a castle, while I have only a box to live in with my twenty-five brothers. That is no place for her. Still, I must try and make her acquaintance.

He hid behind a small box that stood on the table so that he could peep at the little ballerina who continued to stand on one leg without losing her balance. When evening came, the other tin soldiers were all put back in their box and the people of the house went to bed. That's when the toys came to life. They began playing games, paying visits, waging wars, or dancing.

The tin soldiers rattled in their box. They wanted to get out and join the fun, but they could not open the lid. The nutcrackers played leapfrog, and the pencil jumped around on the table. There was so much noise that the canary woke up and began to talk in verse. Only the tin soldier and the dancer remained in their places. She stood on tiptoe as firmly as he did on his one leg. He never took his eyes from her, not for even a moment. The clock struck twelve and, with a bounce, up sprang the lid of a small box and out jumped up a little black goblin—it was a toy puzzle.

"Tin soldier," said the goblin, "don't wish for what does not belong to you."

But the tin soldier pretended not to hear.

"Very well. Wait till tomorrow," said the goblin.

When the children came in the next morning, they placed the tin soldier in the window. Now, whether it was the goblin who did it, or the wind, is not known, but the window flew open and out fell the tin soldier, head over heels, from the third story into the street below. It was a terrible fall. He landed headfirst, with his helmet and his bayonet stuck in between the flagstones, and his one leg up in the air. The servant maid and the little boy went downstairs to look for him, but he was nowhere to be seen. Once they nearly stepped on him. If he had called out, "Here I am," it would have been all right, but he was too proud to cry out for help.

Soon it began to rain. The drops fell faster and faster till there was a heavy shower. When it was over, two boys happened to pass by, and one of them said, "Look, there is a tin soldier. He ought to have a boat to sail in." So they made a boat out of newspaper and placed the tin soldier in it. Then they sent him sailing down the gutter while they ran alongside of it, clapping their hands. Goodness, what large waves there were in that gutter! How fast the water rushed! It had been a very heavy rain and the gutters were full. The paper boat rocked up and down, sometimes turning around so quickly that the tin soldier trembled. But he remained firm. He looked straight ahead and shouldered his rifle. Suddenly the boat shot under a bridge that formed part of a drain. It was as dark as the tin soldier's box.

Where am I going now? he thought. This is the goblin's fault, I'm sure. If only the little ballerina were here with me in the boat, I wouldn't care about the dark.

Just then, a great rat who lived in the drain appeared in front of him.

"Do you have a passport?" asked the rat. "You must give it to me at once."

But the tin soldier remained silent and held his rifle tighter than ever. The boat sailed on and the rat followed it. The rat gnashed his teeth and yelled out, "Stop him, stop him; he has not paid the toll! He has not shown his passport!" But the water rushed on faster and faster. The tin soldier could already see daylight shining where the arch ended. Then he heard a terrible roaring sound. It was enough to frighten even the bravest man. At the end of the tunnel the drain fell straight down into a large canal, which was as dangerous for the tin soldier as a waterfall would be to us. He was too close to it to stop, so the boat rushed on, and the poor tin soldier could only hold himself as stiffly as possible, without moving an eyelid, to show that he was not afraid. The boat whirled around three or four times and then filled with water to the very top. Nothing could save it from sinking. He now stood up to his neck in water, while the boat sank deeper and deeper. The paper became soft and loose till at last the water closed over the soldier's head. He thought of the elegant little dancer whom he should never see again and the words of a song sounded in his ears:

Farewell, warrior! ever brave,
Drifting onward to thy grave.

The paper boat fell to pieces, and the soldier sank into the water where he was immediately swallowed up by a large fish. Oh, how dark it was inside the fish! A great deal darker than in the tunnel and narrower too, but the tin soldier continued firm and lay still, shouldering his rifle. The fish swam to and fro, making the most wonderful movements, but at last he became quite still. After a while, a flash of lightning seemed to pass through him and then the daylight approached, and a voice cried out, "I declare, here is the tin soldier." The fish had been caught, taken to the market, and sold to the cook, who took him into the kitchen and cut him open with a large knife. She picked up the soldier and held him by the waist between her finger and thumb, washed him off, and carried him into the room.

They were all anxious to see this wonderful tin soldier who had traveled inside a fish. They placed him on the table in the very same room where he had begun. There were the same children, the same toys, and standing on the table, the same pretty castle with the elegant little dancer at the door. She still balanced herself on one leg as firmly as he himself. It touched the tin soldier so much to see her that he almost wept tin tears, but he kept them back. He only looked at her, and they both remained silent.

Presently, one of the little boys picked up the tin soldier and threw him into the stove. He had no reason to do this, so it must have been the fault of the goblin who lived in the small box. The flames flickered around the tin

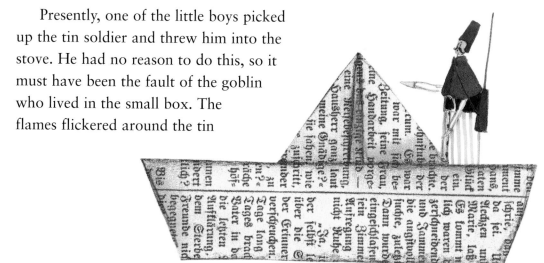

soldier and the heat was terrible. Soon he could see that the bright colors were fading from his uniform. He looked at the little ballerina and she looked at him. He felt himself melting away, but he still remained firm with his gun on his shoulder.

Suddenly the door of the room flew open and a draught of air caught up the little dancer. She fluttered across the room right into the stove beside the tin soldier. She instantly caught fire and was gone. The tin soldier melted down into a lump, and the next morning, when the maid servant took the ashes out of the stove, she found him in the shape of a little tin heart. Nothing remained of the little ballerina but the silver rosette, which was burnt black as cinder.

THE FLYING TRUNK

ONCE UPON A TIME, there was a merchant who was so rich that he could have paved a street with gold and still have had enough for a small alley. But of course he didn't do this. He knew the value of money and would never waste it like that. He was so clever with his money that his investments grew and grew until the day he died. His son inherited his wealth and lived a merry life with it. He went to parties every night, made kites out of money, and threw pieces of gold into the sea, skimming them on the water as if they were stones. And so, he soon lost all his money. At last he had nothing left but a pair of slippers, an old dressing gown, and four small coins. All his friends deserted him. They wouldn't even walk with him in the streets. One of them, who was very good-natured, sent him an old trunk with this message, "Pack up!"

Yes, he thought, it is all very well to say "pack up," but there was nothing left to pack up. So he sat in the trunk himself. It was a wonderful trunk. On a whim, he shut the lid and pressed the lock. As soon as he pressed the lock, the trunk began to fly. The trunk flew up the chimney with the merchant's son in it! It flew right up into the clouds. When the bottom of the trunk began to creak, the son was frightened. He knew if the trunk fell apart, he would likely fall to his death.

However, he soon arrived safely in Turkey. He hid the trunk in the woods under some dry leaves and went into a nearby town. No one noticed him, for the Turks also dressed in dressing gowns and slippers, as he did. He soon met a nanny with a little child. "I say," he cried, "what castle is that near town, with the windows placed so high?"

"The king's daughter lives there," the nanny replied. "It has been foretold that she will be very unhappy in love. So no one is allowed to visit her, unless the king and queen are present."

"Thank you," said the merchant's son. Then he went back to the woods, seated himself in his trunk, flew up to the roof of the castle, and crept through a window into the princess's room. She lay on the bed asleep. She was so beautiful that the merchant's son could not help but kiss her. When she awoke, she was very frightened. But he told her he was a Turkish angel who had come down through the air to see her. This pleased her very much. He sat down by her side and talked to her. He said her eyes were like beautiful dark lakes where her thoughts swam about like little mermaids. He told her that her forehead was a snowy mountain with splendid halls full of pictures. And then he told her a story about a stork who brings beautiful children from the rivers. These were delightful stories, and when he asked the princess if she would marry him, she consented immediately.

"But you must come on Saturday," she said, "for then the king and queen will take tea with me. They will be very proud when they find I am going to marry a Turkish angel. You must think of some pretty stories to tell them, for my parents like to hear stories better than anything. My mother prefers ones that are deep and have morals; but my father likes funny stories that make him laugh."

"Very well," he replied. "I shall bring you nothing more than a story," and so they parted. However, the princess gave him a sword that was studded with gold coins, and these he could use.

He flew to town and bought a new dressing gown and then returned to the woods, where he began to write a story so he would be ready for Saturday. It was not an easy task. However, by Saturday, when he went to see the princess, the story was finished. The king, the queen, and the whole court were at tea with the princess when he arrived, and he was politely received.

"Will you tell us a story?" asked the queen. "Preferably one that is instructive and full of deep learning."

"Yes, but with something in it to laugh at as well," said the king.

"Certainly," he replied, and he began at once, asking them first to listen carefully.

"There was once a bundle of matches that were exceedingly proud of their high

position. Their genealogical tree, that is, a large pine tree from which they had been cut, was at one time a large, old tree in the woods. The matches now lay between a tinderbox and an old iron saucepan and were talking about their youthful days.

'Ah! Then we grew on the green boughs and were as green as they were. Every morning and evening we were fed with diamond drops of dew. When the sun shone, we felt his warm rays and the little birds would relate stories to us as they sang. We knew that we were rich, for the other trees only wore their green dress in summer, but our family was able to array themselves in green summer and winter. Then the woodcutter came and our family fell under his axe. The head of the house obtained a position as mainmast in a very fine ship and sails around the world. The other branches of the family were taken to different places, and our job now is to kindle a light for common people. This is how such high-born people as we came to be in a kitchen.'

'Mine was a very different fate,' said the iron pot that stood by the matches. 'From my first entrance into the world I have been used to cooking and scouring. I am the first used in this house when anything solid or useful is required. My greatest pleasure is to be made clean and shining after dinner and to sit in my place and have a sensible conversation with my neighbors. All of us, except for the water bucket, which is sometimes taken into the courtyard, live here together within these four walls. We get our news from the market basket, but he sometimes tells us very unpleasant things about the people and the government. Yes, and one day an old pot was so alarmed at one of the stories that he fell down and broke into pieces.'

'You talk too much,' said the tinderbox.

'Yes, of course,' said the matches. 'Let us talk about those who are the highest born.'

'No, let us think of some other amusement,' said the saucepan. 'I will begin. We will tell something that has happened to us. That will be very easy and interesting as well. On the Baltic Sea, near the Danish shore . . .'

'What a pretty start!' said the plates. 'We shall all like this story, I am sure.'

'Yes, well, in my youth, I lived in a quiet family, where the furniture was polished, the floors scrubbed, and clean curtains put up every month.'

'What an interesting way you have of telling a story,' said the carpet broom.

'That is quite true,' said the water bucket, and he jumped a little with joy, splashing some water on the floor.

The saucepan went on with his story, and the end was as good as the beginning.

The plates rattled with pleasure, and the carpet broom brought some green parsley out of the dust-bin and crowned the saucepan, for he knew it would vex the others and besides, he thought, If I crown him today he will crown me tomorrow.

'Now, let us dance,' said the firetongs; and how they danced, with one leg stuck up in the air. The chair cushion in the corner burst with laughter when she saw it.

'Shall I be crowned now?' asked the firetongs; so the broom found another wreath for the tongs.

'They are only common people after all,' thought the matches.

The teapot was now asked to sing, but she said she had a cold and could not sing without boiling water. They all thought this was just an excuse because she did not want to sing anywhere except in the parlor, when she sat on the table with the grand people.

In the window sat an old quill pen that the maid generally wrote with. There was nothing remarkable about the pen, except that it had been dipped too deeply in the ink, but it was proud of that.

'If the teapot won't sing,' said the pen, 'there is a nightingale in a cage who can sing. She doesn't know much, certainly, but we need not say anything about that this evening.'

'I think it highly improper,' said the teakettle, who was the kitchen singer and half brother to the teapot, 'that a rich foreign bird should sing here. Is it patriotic? Let the market basket decide what is right.'

'I certainly am vexed,' said the basket, 'inwardly vexed, more than anyone can imagine. Are we spending the evening properly? Wouldn't it be more sensible to put the house in order? If each of us were in his own place I could lead us all in a game.'

'Let us act a play,' they all said. At that very moment, the door opened and the maid came in. No one stirred; they all remained perfectly still. Yet, at the same time, there was not a single pot among them who didn't have a high opinion of himself and of what he could do if he so chose.

Yes, if we had chosen to, they each thought, we might have spent a very pleasant evening.

The maid took the matches and lit them. Dear me, how they sputtered and flared up!

Now then, they thought, everyone will see that we are the first. See how we shine! What a light we give! But even while they spoke, their light went out.

"What a wonderful story," said the queen. "I feel as if I were really in the kitchen and could see the matches. Yes, you shall marry our daughter."

"Certainly," said the king, "thou shalt have our daughter." The king said *thou* to him because he was going to be one of the family. The wedding day was set and, on the evening before, the whole city was lit up. Cakes and sweets were thrown

among the people. The street boys stood on tiptoe and shouted *hurrah!* and whistled between their fingers. It was a very splendid affair.

"I will give them another treat," said the merchant's son. So he bought rockets and firecrackers and all sorts of fireworks, packed them in his trunk, and flew up with it into the air. What a whizzing and popping they made as they went off! The Turks, when they saw such a sight, jumped so high that their slippers flew about their ears. It was easy to believe after this that the princess really was going to marry a Turkish angel.

As soon as the merchant's son had come down in his flying trunk to the woods after the fireworks, he thought, I will go back into town now and hear what they think of the entertainment. It was natural that he should wish to know. And what strange things people said! Everyone he questioned had a different tale to tell, though they all thought it very beautiful.

"I saw the Turkish angel myself," said one. "He had eyes like glittering stars and a head like foaming water."

"He flew in a mantle of fire," cried another, "with lovely little cherubs peeping out from the folds."

He heard many more fine things about himself, including that the next day he was to be married. After this, he went back to the forest to rest in his trunk. But it had disappeared! A spark from one of the firecrackers had set it on fire. It was burned to ashes! So the merchant's son could not fly anymore or go to meet his bride.

She stood all day on the roof waiting for him and most likely she is waiting there still, while he wanders through the world telling fairy tales. However, none of them are as amusing as the one he told about the matches.

JACK THE DULLARD

FAR AWAY in the country, there was an old inn run by an old man who had two sons. These two young men thought themselves to be quite clever. More than anything else, they wanted to go out and woo the king's daughter. The maiden in question had publicly announced that she would choose as her husband the young man who was best able to speak.

So they set to the task of getting ready for their quest. They only had a week, but they were sure that would be enough time, for they had already accumulated a lot of information, and everyone knows how useful that is.

One of them knew the whole Latin dictionary by heart, as well as three whole years of the daily newspaper of their little town. He knew it so well that he could repeat it all backward or forward, just as he chose. The other was well read in law, and, accordingly, he thought he could talk of affairs of state and put his spoke in the wheel of the council. And he knew one thing more— he could embroider suspenders with roses and other flowers and with arabesques, for he was a truly light-fingered fellow.

"I shall win the princess!" they both declared. And so, their old papa gave each of them a handsome horse. The youth who knew the dictionary and newspaper by heart received a black horse, and the one who knew all about the law received a milk-white steed. They rubbed the corners of their mouths with fish oil, so that they would be very smooth and glib. The servants stood below in the courtyard and looked on while they mounted their horses. Just by chance the third son arrived, for the innkeeper actually had three sons, though nobody counted the third along with his brothers because he was not so learned as they, and indeed he was generally known as Jack the Dullard.

"Hello!" said Jack. "Where are you going in your Sunday best?"

"We're going to the king's court, as suitors to the king's daughter. Haven't you heard about the announcement that has been made throughout the country?" And they told him all about it.

"My word! I'll go too!" cried Jack. His two brothers burst out laughing and rode away.

"Father, dear," said Jack, "I must have a horse too. I do feel so desperately inclined to marry! If she accepts me, she accepts me, and she shall be mine!"

"Don't talk nonsense," replied the old man. "You shall get no horse from me. You don't know how to speak. You can't even arrange your words. Your brothers are very different from you."

"Well," said Jack, "if I can't have a horse, I'll take my billy goat. He can carry me very well!"

And so said, so done. He mounted the billy goat, pressed his heels into its sides, and galloped down the high street like a hurricane.

"Giddyup! What a ride! Here I come!" shouted Jack, and he sang till his voice echoed far and wide. But his brothers rode slowly on ahead of him. They spoke not a word, for they were thinking about the fine speeches they would soon have to give, and these had to be cleverly prepared beforehand.

"Hello!" shouted Jack. "Here am I! Look what I have found on the road." And he showed them. It was a dead crow.

"Dullard!" exclaimed his brothers. "What are you going to do with that?"

"With the crow? Why, I am going to give it to the princess."

"Yes, you should do that," said they and they laughed, and rode on.

"Hello, here I am again! See what I have found now! You sure don't find things like this on the high street every day!"

And the brothers turned round to see what he could have found now.

"Dullard!" they cried. "That is only an old wooden shoe and the upper part is missing in the bargain. Are you going to give that to the princess as well?"

"Most certainly I shall," replied Jack, and again his brothers laughed and rode on, and soon they were far ahead of him.

"Hello, giddyup!" There was Jack again. "It is getting better and better," he cried. "Hurrah!"

"Why, what have you found this time?" inquired the brothers.

"Oh," said Jack, "I can hardly wait to tell you. How glad the princess will be!"

"Bah!" said his brothers. "That is nothing but clay from the ditch."

"Yes, certainly it is," said Jack, "and clay of the finest sort. See? It is so wet, it runs through one's fingers." And he filled his pocket with the clay.

His brothers galloped on till the sparks flew from their horses' hooves, and they arrived at the town gate a full hour earlier than Jack. Now, at the gate, each suitor was provided with a number and was placed in a row of six suitors per row. They were so closely packed together that they could not move their arms, and that was a prudent arrangement, for had they been able, they would certainly have come to blows, merely because one of them stood before the other.

All the inhabitants of the country stood in great crowds around the castle to see the princess receive the suitors, and as each stepped into the hall, his power of speech seemed to desert him, like the light of a candle that is blown out. Then the princess would say, "He won't do! Away with him!"

At last the turn came for the brother who knew the dictionary by heart; but he did not know it now, he had absolutely forgotten it altogether, and the floorboards seemed to echo with his footsteps, and the ceiling of the hall was made of mirrors so that he seemed to be standing on his head. At the window stood three clerks and a head clerk, and every one of them was writing down every single word that was uttered, so that it might be printed in the newspapers and sold for a penny on the street corners. It was a terrible ordeal. Furthermore, the fire in the stove in that room seemed quite red-hot.

"It is dreadfully hot in here!" observed the first brother.

"Yes," replied the princess, "my father is going to roast young pullets today."

"Baa!" There he stood, helpless as a lamb. He had not been prepared for a speech of this kind and had not a word to say, and though he intended to say something witty, he could only repeat, "Baa!"

"He won't do!" said the princess. "Away with him!"

And he was obliged to go.

And now the second brother came in. "It is terribly warm in here!" he observed.

"Yes, we're roasting pullets today," replied the princess.

"What, what were you, were you pleased to ob . . ." he stammered as the clerks wrote it all down, ". . . pleased to ob . . ."

"He won't do!" said the princess. "Away with him!"

Now came the turn of Jack the Dullard. He rode into the hall on his goat.

"Well, it is most abominably hot in here."

"Yes, because I'm roasting young pullets," replied the princess.

"Ah, that's lucky!" exclaimed Jack. "For I suppose you'll let me roast my crow at the same time?"

"With the greatest pleasure," said the princess. "But have you anything you can roast it in? For I have neither pot nor pan."

"Certainly I have!" said Jack. "Here's a cooking utensil."

And he brought out the old wooden shoe and put the crow into it.

"Well, that is an interesting dish!" said the princess. "But what shall we do for sauce?"

"Oh, I have that in my pocket," said Jack. "I have so much of it that I can afford to throw some away." And he poured some of the clay out of his pocket.

"I like that!" said the princess. "You can give an answer, you have something to say for yourself, and so you shall be my husband. But are you aware that every word we speak is being taken down and will be published in the paper tomorrow?"

She only said this to frighten Jack, and the clerks laughed so hard that each one squirted a blot of ink from their pens onto the floor.

"Oh, those are the gentlemen, are they?" said Jack. "I will give the best I have to the head clerk." And he turned out his pockets and flung the wet clay full in the head clerk's face.

"That was very cleverly done," observed the princess. "I could not have done that; but I shall learn in time."

And so Jack the Dullard was made a king and received a crown and a wife and sat upon a throne. And we have this report still hot from the press of the head clerk—although he is not to be depended upon in the least.

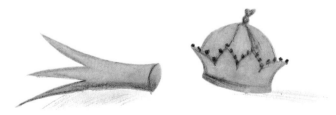

HANS CHRISTIAN ANDERSEN was born April 2, 1805, in Odense, Denmark, the son of a poor shoemaker. As an adult, Andersen traveled widely throughout Europe, Africa, and Turkey, and his stories are flavored with what he saw and experienced.

Andersen worked as an actor, playwright, and illustrator, and was a master silhouette maker. But he remains best known around the world for his fairy tales, of which there are approximately 170.

Andersen died on August 4, 1875, in Copenhagen, Denmark.

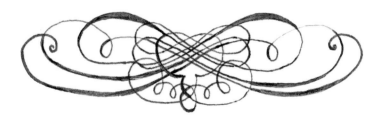